The Wish Maker

The Billionaires of Silicon Forest, Book Two

MELISSA McCLONE

The Wish Maker
The Billionaires of Silicon Forest (Book 2)
Copyright © 2019 Melissa McClone

Cover by Elizabeth Mackay

Cardinal Press, LLC
December 2019
ISBN-13: 9781944777692

Dedication

To all the wish makers out there.
Never stop wishing!

Special thanks to:
Julie Trettel for being keeping me going when I wanted to stop and telling me I could finish the book when I had my doubts. Las Vegas, Houston, I can't wait to see where we end up together next!

Shari Bartholomew for
answering my hospital questions.

Jennifer Niles for helping figure
out foundation donations.

And to my team for being so flexible when life got crazy and in the way: When We Share, It's Your Story Content Editing, Rebecca Hodges, Judy's Proofreading, Deaton Author Services, Finishing Touch Editing, The Word Fairy, The Beta Buddy, and Essentially Chas. You all are the best. Thank you so much for all you do for me!

Chapter One

In his office, Weston E. Lockhart IV sat behind his desk. Considering his company had a paperless environment initiative, he hadn't expected to be handed a stack of manila folders. "Going old school on me?"

Sadie Sanchez's smile spread to her warm brown eyes. The savvy woman who ran his philanthropic foundation was as intelligent as she was dedicated. "I figured you'd want to read the actual thank-you cards and letters instead of digital copies."

Each week, she forwarded emails from those receiving donations from his foundation, both non-profits and individuals. Wes enjoyed reading what she sent, but the cards were his favorite because those took more effort and time to send. As his late grandmother and he sipped tea when he was growing up, she'd instilled writing thank-you notes during one of her many etiquette lessons. He'd smiled then, laughing to himself at the practice, but now, he understood. Physically holding on to something connected him to the foundation's recipients in a way words on a screen couldn't.

Wes grinned. "You know me well."

She patted her round stomach. "Which gives me job security despite baby number three arriving in January."

Each pregnancy, Sadie showed sooner, and her belly got bigger. Not that Wes would say either of those things to her.

"A few included children's drawings," she added. "You should be proud of yourself. You made a huge difference in these people's lives."

"You and your team did the legwork." These days, Wes preferred to stay in the background, sending others to attend charity events in the foundation's name. "I just signed the check."

"You'll have more to sign soon. The first batch of holiday disbursements is almost ready for your John Hancock." Sadie's expression softened. "Quadrupling the Christmas donations this year is an amazing gesture. Next to you, Santa will look like a slacker."

Emotion clogged Wes's throat. Not amazing. His gesture was one hundred percent selfish. He'd stared at his reflection in the mirror and not liked what he saw—thirty-five years of entitlement and selfishness.

But he wanted to change that.

Was trying to change.

Twelve months ago, his life had been in flux—in turmoil—because of the cancer. Hodgkin's lymphoma was treatable, yes, and his had finally—thankfully—responded to treatment, but that didn't mean the diagnosis hadn't terrified him or that he could stop worrying the cancer would return. He'd gone from thinking of growing old to thinking of his life expectancy in five-year increments.

But he was in remission.

Remission.

He enjoyed saying and thinking that word.

Wes had been given the opportunity to do more and be a better person. He regretted being known as a businessman who didn't care who he trampled on to get what he wanted, but he would change that. Step one was to make the holidays merry and bright for others. Many needed a second chance, too. Sometimes a third and fourth one. He could provide that.

"Thanks." Wes forced out the word. "Just doing my part."

"You do more than that. We did good work before, but the foundation is making a profound impact these days. Which is why I love my job even more."

Sadie was the driving force behind the

foundation, and no matter how many kids she and her husband had, the job would be hers for however long she wanted it. "I'll miss you while you're on leave."

She swished her hand through the air as if brushing away his words. "My team is the best. You won't know I'm gone."

"At least not until a member of your team emails digital copies of the thank-you notes," he joked.

"I'll tell them to pass on the actual letters to you."

Without Sadie and the foundation, his reputation would be in far worse shape. "Appreciate it."

Her smile wavered.

That was unusual. "What?"

"You won't like what I have to say."

Probably not if she was warning him, but… "When has that stopped you?"

"Never." She took a breath and then exhaled loudly. "Chairpersons keep calling. They want to know if you'll be representing the foundation at their Christmas events and galas."

Wes sighed. Sadie had a master's in public administration. She didn't need to be acting as his social secretary. "If anyone calls again, refer them to Eliza."

Eliza Culpepper, his personal assistant, had worked for his father before Wes took over as CEO. Behind her grandmotherly voice and twinkling blue eyes was a hard-nosed, take-no-prisoners executive assistant who had kept Wes and his company from falling apart after his diagnosis.

"I don't mind," Sadie replied sincerely.

"I do." He shook his head. "They only want to appease their curiosity about my post-cancer appearance and who I'm dating now."

Sadie's brows drew together. "I thought you were taking a break from dating."

"I am, but they don't know that."

Wes wanted to keep it that way. His private life used to be splashed across the internet and society pages, but he guarded his privacy these days. A hard lesson learned.

"You should attend one event," Sadie encouraged. "People would love to see you. They miss you."

"They miss my checkbook and credit card."

"The foundation takes care of that whether or not you're at a function," she countered.

True, but… "They've survived without my sparkling personality for two years. Another won't matter."

Amusement gleamed in Sadie's gaze. "You mean your grizzly personality, right?"

He growled.

She laughed. "If you go, you'll have your choice from a bevy of beauties wanting to be your plus-one for the evening."

Those women were only interested in one thing—his money. Which was why Wes would rather spend time at his lodge in Hood Hamlet on Mount Hood or in Portland with friends.

In the past, he hadn't cared why a woman had wanted to go out with him. The time together had been mutually beneficial. Until Annabelle…

Nope.

Not going there.

The memories—and the emotions they dredged up—belonged in the past.

Or forgotten completely.

"I'll keep that in mind," he said in a matter-of-fact tone.

"No, you won't," Sadie teased. "But I had to try."

"Duly noted." He glanced at the folders. "Anything else?"

"Not until the next batch of checks is ready."

"See you then."

Sadie rubbed her lower back.

Worry shot through him. Wes jumped to his feet. "Are you okay? Do you need a doctor?"

She massaged the same spot. "I'll be fine once this soon-to-be nine-pound bowling ball is out of me. At least this one doesn't kick as hard as the first two. Those feet and elbows against internal organs caught me off guard more than once."

Wes cringed. He didn't even want to imagine that.

Telling Sadie to go home was on the tip of his tongue, but if he did, she would lecture him on pregnancy not being an illness. "Take care of yourself."

"Always, boss." She left his office, closing the door behind her.

Wes returned to his chair, sat, and opened the folder on top to find an unopened envelope. That was odd. Sadie's team usually sorted through the mail. His name had been handwritten on the front. The return address was local, but one he didn't recognize.

After opening the envelope, he removed two sheets of paper and unfolded them. The letter was handwritten, not typed.

Dear Wes,

It was so nice to put a face to your name at the funeral, though I wish the circumstances could have been better. Zeke mentioned you so many times over the past two years. My husband never thought a fellow patient he met in Dr. Regis's waiting room would become a friend, but that is what he called you. His friend. One who understood what he was going through as no one else could.

I can't thank you enough for paying Zeke's funeral costs, his medical bills, and establishing education funds for our two kids. No matter how much you plan for a worst-case scenario, it's never enough.

But thanks to you, I have less to worry about now. I know Zeke is smiling down from heaven with a told-you-it-would-all-work-out smirk on his face.

A thank you can never describe my appreciation and relief knowing the twins can now attend whatever college they want.

Maybe they'll end up wearing your Cardinal red or perhaps they'll follow in their dad's footsteps to become a Duck. Though if I have my way, they'll be in Pullman. Go Cougs!

I'm so grateful for all you did for Zeke and now for us. I hope your generosity and kindness are repaid tenfold. And that good health and happiness are showered upon you.

Zeke worried about you. He thought you might feel guilty when you went into remission and he didn't. I hope that's not the case, but please know, he was so relieved you beat this thing. Truly. You being in remission gave him hope that the same might happen for him. And he needed that hope. We all did.

This letter has gone on far longer than I intended. But thank you from the bottom of my heart. My husband was a man of few words, but I know he would say the same thing, too. I hope you have the merriest of Christmases, Wes, and that you find whatever you wish for under the tree on the twenty-fifth!

Thanks again,
Melanie Dwyer

Wes's hands trembled. His eyes burned. He blinked before rereading the letter. Zeke, an engineer for a local semiconductor company, had become a good friend, albeit an unexpected one. No wonder Sadie and her team hadn't opened this letter. The foundation wasn't involved with this gift, only Wes.

He rubbed his face and then slid the letter into the file. He would put this one in his office at home.

As he opened the next folder, his desk phone

buzzed. He picked up the receiver. "Lockhart."

"Henry is on his way in," Eliza announced in her no-nonsense tone. "He promised to be brief."

Henry Davenport, an eccentric billionaire extraordinaire, had a different definition of the word than most people. But if anyone could make Wes smile, Henry could. The guy was thirty-three, but at times acted more like a thirteen-year-old. They'd known each other for as long as Wes could remember, but became close friends after Henry, two years younger than him, graduated college. Both were the only sons of two old-money families in Portland. But for as much as Wes worked, Henry played. "Make sure I'm not late for my next meeting."

Even if the last thing Wes wanted to discuss was the acquisition of NanoNeu.

"I'll drag you out of there even if Henry wants to play tug-of-war with you as the rope."

Ouch. That would hurt, but Wes could see both people enjoying the battle. "Let's hope it doesn't come to that."

"Three, two, one…"

The door to Wes's office flew open. Henry entered, carrying a black garment bag and bringing with him a high energy that could either be contagious or draining. He wore a gray plaid suit that was more appropriate for Fashion Week in New York, London, Paris, or Milan than a Wednesday in Portland. Typical Henry. The guy could be a model, but that would mean showing up for a shoot on time. Not possible because setting an alarm took too much effort.

"It's such a beautiful December day in the Pacific Northwest." Henry approached the desk. "And yours just got brighter."

Wes leaned back in his chair. "Why is that?"

"Because I'm here."

He should have realized that. In Henry's mind, the world revolved around him. That included friends and strangers. Still, Wes was curious about the impromptu visit. Henry only dropped by if they were meeting for lunch. "It's early afternoon, so I'm sure you've eaten already. Why are you here?"

Henry grinned like the Cheshire cat. "I have something for you."

His gifts ranged from the extravagant to the exotic, but they were always heartfelt. Henry had no family except the one he'd created with his friends, and he cherished each of those people, Wes included.

Wes figured he had a fifty percent chance of guessing correctly. "In the garment bag?"

"I can't pull anything over on you brainy tech guys." Henry unzipped the bag and pulled out a…

Wes did a double take. Blinked. No, he hadn't been seeing things. "Is that a—"

"Yes, it is."

Scratching his chin, Wes stared at the Santa suit hanging from a wooden hanger. The thick pure white trim, luxurious red velvet fabric, and wide black leather belt screamed top-of-the-line quality. Not that he expected anything less than Kris Kringle bespoke from his friend, but his you-know-why-I'm-here expression irritated Wes, who hadn't a clue what Henry was up to this time.

The guy was most likely being his irreverent self—a fun-seeking, man-child—and nothing serious was wrong, but Wes had to ask. "What are you doing here with a Santa suit?"

"This is not 'a' Santa suit. It belongs to me. Custom-made." Henry picked a piece of lint off the sleeve. "I'm not sure the big man at the North Pole has one as nice as mine."

Wes rolled his eyes. No doubt Henry's multibillion-dollar net worth without having worked a day in his life made him believe in Santa Claus, the Easter Bunny, and the Tooth Fairy. Given he threw a birthday party for himself each year on April Fools' Day and made a big deal out of others who had holiday birthdays, it wouldn't surprise Wes.

He leaned forward. "You haven't answered my question."

"I'm getting there." Henry's mouth slanted. "I brought the suit for you to wear. I'll want it back, of course. Sweet little Noelle will expect her godfather to wear it on Christmas morning."

Of course, but what Henry said clarified nothing. Very Henry.

"It may be December," Wes said. "But red isn't

my color."

"Funny, Lockhart."

Wes pushed up his cuff to check the time on his watch. "I have a meeting in ten minutes. Tell me why I need your Santa suit."

Lines creased Henry's forehead. "Because of what you said at Blaise and Hadley's wedding."

"I was the best man. I said a lot." Especially after a few glasses of champagne.

"It was after Dash caught the garter."

Another mutual friend of theirs Dash Cabot, aka Wonderkid of Silicon Forest, had worn the garter around his bicep like a badge of honor. The one who'd been the most thrilled, however, had been his plus-one, Raina. Diamond solitaires and platinum wedding bands had shone in her eyes the rest of the reception.

"That was a month ago." The thirty days had passed glacier-forming slow for Wes.

Dash was still dating Raina, but he appeared to be in no hurry to take the relationship to the next level. Typical for Mr. Status Quo, another one of Dash's nicknames, but a bummer for Wes that Dash wasn't getting serious more quickly. Once Dash married, Wes would win the last-single-man-standing bet he'd made with his friends years ago. The prize—an investment fund now worth over five hundred million dollars and bragging rights. The latter meant more to him, but everyone—well, the five other men in the bet, Henry, and another mutual friend Brett Matthews—assumed Wes wanted the money.

"Remind me," Wes said.

"You said you wanted to make the most of the holiday season by giving back, paying it forward, whatever you want to call it."

The champagne must have loosened Wes's tongue. He hadn't meant to make a big announcement like that. Not even in front of his closest friends. "I did, and I do, but—"

Henry raised his hand to stop Wes. "Your way of helping is to have your foundation make a donation and be done with it."

Shame sliced through Wes. That was exactly what he planned to do. What Sadie and her team had been doing. Well, except for Zeke's family, but that was different. "People need money."

Henry sighed as if the emergency broadcast system had just warned of a massive meteor hurtling to earth. "Yes, and a donation, particularly the size your foundation makes, can be life-changing for a group or a person, but people also need the personal touch, especially around the holidays. To know someone cares."

"I care." If Wes didn't, he wouldn't do anything other than make the requisite donations per his accountant's recommendations—an amount far less than their goal this year. "But giving money works better with my schedule."

Henry's gaze narrowed. "You've cut back on your hours."

"I have." Work was no longer Wes's priority, but he wanted to help without being personally involved. Nothing wrong with that. "But wearing a Santa suit implies making an appearance somewhere. Giving money is easier."

Henry cocked a brow. "When did you start choosing the easier path?"

A valid question given Wes's past, but he wasn't that same man. He never wanted to be him again.

Even though Wes was in remission, he was still recovering from the stress and strain of the treatments, the uncertainty of wondering if he'd live to see another Christmas or birthday, the fear his legacy would be known for dismantling companies to grow his own.

Wes raised his chin. "When I realized how precious life is. It's meant to be enjoyed, not spent increasing the bottom line and making more work for myself."

"I understand, and I'm happy you see that now." Henry spoke sincerely. "But you must play Santa. The patients at the children's hospital will appreciate you being at their holiday party even if money is a more practical way to help."

Okay, Henry's visit made sense now. The guy had donated the wing that housed the well-regarded children's hospital in honor of his late parents. No wonder he burst into the office like a rabid elf on a critical mission. That, however, didn't change Wes's mind. "Ask Brett or one of the other guys."

Although Wes could only picture Brett in the red suit with kids climbing all over him. No one else in their group was a dad.

"Brett is my backup choice," Henry admitted. "You, my old friend, are my number one pick. Not all the kids have cancer, but you understand what these kids are going through. You'll know what to say."

No way. Wes pushed away from his desk to put more distance between him and Henry.

Wes didn't have a clue what to say to sick kids. Not when he could barely help himself. He still freaked out when he felt tired or sick, fearing the cancer had returned. His therapist claimed that was a normal reaction. Nothing Wes had been through was normal. "I'm sorry, but I'm not the right person for this."

Henry studied Wes. "When were you last at the hospital?"

He hadn't been back since a scan months ago. "It's been a while."

"Then this is the perfect time for you to visit," Henry said without missing a beat. "You can say hello to people you know. Wish them a 'Merry Christmas' and spread holiday cheer."

"I don't want to do this."

Henry shrugged. "There are times we need to do

things we'd rather not do."

Uh-oh. Wes recognized Henry's tone. That meant two things—trouble and defeat.

Wes slumped. "You're not going to give up on this."

"I'll never give up on you, Wes." Mischief filled Henry's eyes. "And I'm only getting started with this, but you have a meeting."

For once, Wes was grateful for an overscheduled day. "I do."

"I'll leave the suit here. A reminder for you to think about what I asked." Henry returned the suit to its bag, zipped it up, and laid it across a chair. "The Christmas party is on the eighth at four o'clock. I checked with Eliza. You're free, so she's tentatively marked it on your schedule."

Tentatively, right?

No doubt he told Eliza to use a permanent marker.

Wes sighed.

Knowing Henry, he hadn't set the date and time until he'd known Wes was available. "You think of everything."

"I try, but Rachael Reese is planning the event, so she's the brains behind this party."

Rachael was Mason Reese's wife, another one of the six friends known as the Billionaires of Silicon Forest. Mason and Rachael's wedding in early September had knocked him out of the running to win the last-man-single-standing bet, but Mason seemed happy being married.

Lucky him.

Blaise, Adam, and Kieran, too.

Wes could have been like them, if not for…

"Playing Santa will be easy," Henry said. "I promise."

Wes stared at the garment bag. "When do you need an answer?"

"By tomorrow." Henry grinned. "Not that this decision should require much thought. No money is involved. Only time."

"Time is money."

"In this instance, time is caring. And it'll be good to visit the hospital when it's your choice and not something forced on you by your health." Henry's challenge was clear.

"I'm not afraid to go there." The words shot out of Wes's mouth.

"If you say so."

Wes squared his shoulders. "I do."

"Excellent." Henry beamed. "Then there's nothing stopping you from saying yes."

"I—"

"I don't want to face Eliza's wrath and make you late for your meeting. Be at the hospital in the Santa suit at a little after four. That way you, as the guest of honor, can make a grand entrance."

With that, Henry breezed out of the office as if

he'd never been there. Well, except for the Santa suit he'd left behind.

How did Henry always get what he wanted?

Dumbfounded, Wes's gaze traveled from the empty doorway to the garment bag. There appeared to be boots inside, too. And yes, he and Henry wore the same shoe size.

Wes blew out a breath. "Guess I'd better start practicing my ho-ho-hos."

Chapter Two

Dr. Paige Regis stood at the fifth-floor nurses' station, replying to emails from patients before it got too late. Light brown strands of hair hung in her face. She pushed them aside. As soon as she finished, she could fix her ponytail.

Not that anyone was around to notice her.

She hadn't meant to stay at the hospital this long, but during rounds, a patient and her husband needed answers to their questions. Then, one of her pediatric hematology-oncology counterparts had asked Paige to stop by to consult on his young-adult patient, a soccer player, so here she was.

On a Saturday night.

Story of her life.

But she didn't mind.

Being here was her job.

It wasn't as if anyone was at home waiting for her. Which was why she had no pets. Over half a dozen succulents had died. One philodendron, who she'd named Phil, remained alive, but those were hard to kill. Which meant Paige's thumb wasn't green, and she was better at caring for patients than houseplants.

Elise, a second-shift RN, rounded the corner and then sat behind the counter. "It's nice to have more than a minute to get off my feet."

"Slow night?"

"Not really, but it's not crazy like it can be." Elise's gaze traveled from the clock to Paige. "No big date?"

If only.

Casual dating didn't do much for Paige. She dreamed about falling in love, getting married, and having a family, but the timing had been wrong each time she thought she'd met her future husband. "Nope."

"Weren't you dating some guy?"

"That was a couple months ago." Though "some guy" described her exes perfectly.

Her college boyfriend had broken up with her a week before graduation after meeting someone else. The next guy, a med student like herself, headed to the East Coast for his residency while hers was out West. Their long-distance relationship lasted six months before they mutually decided it wasn't working. The men she'd dated since then were nice, but none had led to a forever kind of love—or even a serious relationship—for one reason or another.

No one's fault.

Just life.

And her job because of the hours she worked.

Paige joked to friends if she found a man who understood her drive and determination, didn't mind how much she worked, and supported her endeavors, she would marry him on the spot. So far that hadn't happened.

Not even close.

Still, work fulfilled her. She was in her element, thriving on problem-solving and keeping up with the cutting-edge research. Her job kept her from being lonely. As did the belief her single status would eventually change, and she would find a partner—a husband—to love. Even if she'd recently turned thirty-seven, there was no need to freak out about being perpetually single or research her options for having a baby on her own.

There was still time.

"Swipe right and see what happens," Elise suggested.

"I tried the dating apps and deleted them." Paige wanted a relationship, which required meeting men and going out to see if they were compatible, but there had to be a better way. "Maybe I'll try again in the new year, but tonight, I'm looking forward to a date with my television and whatever Christmas movie is on when I get home."

"I set my DVR to record movies today so I can binge watch on my days off."

"I've had mine recording since the new ones premiered."

"Great minds…" Elise grinned. "Have you started your Christmas shopping yet?"

"No, but I plan to start and finish tomorrow by buying everything online. I'll have the presents wrapped and shipped with a couple of clicks."

Paige's family was gathering at her brother's house in Vermont for the holidays, but she was on call so she was staying home. It wouldn't be her first Christmas alone. She would put up a tree, hang a stocking, and string lights along her condo's windows. She'd preordered a holiday meal from the grocery store that would leave her plenty of leftovers.

"That way I can avoid the crowds and parking woes at the mall," she added.

Elise's nose scrunched. "Yes, but you won't be able to buy yourself an impromptu present if something catches your eye or ooh and ahh at the shiny decorations."

"I'll order myself a present." A new fleece throw or a pair of fuzzy slippers or a set of bath bombs might be nice. Maybe she'd buy all three and have them wrapped so she would have more than her family's gifts to open on Christmas morning. "And we have decorations here."

Only a week into December and this floor was decked for the holidays with garlands, lights, and red bows, giving the place a festive feel for the staff, their young patients, and the family members who came to visit.

Elise motioned to the artificial tree decorated with multicolored lights. Silver and gold bells—big enough that smaller mouths couldn't swallow them—hung from the branches. "Our repeat customers have been eyeing the bells."

By the time the twenty-fifth arrived, few—if any—bells would remain because one was given with a patient's discharge paperwork. Paige enjoyed the tradition and had suggested it for their cancer care unit in the main hospital next door. "They must remember from last year."

Elise nodded. "But even the new ones are curious."

"They'll figure it out soon enough."

Imagining children ringing their bell on the way out of the hospital filled Paige with warmth. A few said they were giving angels their wings. Others claimed to be spreading the spirit of Christmas. No matter the reason, the bells brought smiles, and that was what counted.

"Dr. Regis," a familiar female voice called out.

"Good luck," Elise muttered under her breath before scurrying away.

As Paige pasted on a smile, Amanda West—the hospital administrator—approached at a quick pace. The woman was in her early fifties. Her almost black hair was cut in a severe bob with sharp ends that could take someone's eye out if they didn't keep their distance. She wore pants with a coordinating blazer every day, whether it was summer or winter.

"Working late?" Paige asked, surprised to see Amanda on a Saturday night.

"I want to speak with you." Amanda's serious tone matched her gaze. She was to the point and often blunt, but each year under her leadership, the hospital's ranking and prestige rose. "Since your office is closed on Saturdays, I assumed you would be here."

Paige swallowed a sigh. Guess her routine had become predictable. Nothing she could do about that. "What's up?"

"Funding for the cancer center came up twenty-five million short."

Her heart plummeted. The cancer center was her project—her passion. "I thought we had enough."

Amanda pursed her lips. "We did. Now we don't."

Paige started to speak but stopped herself because she had no idea what to say. Construction on the new building was supposed to begin in the new year. Any delays would have a cascading effect.

A negative one.

"Don't look so sad." Amanda lowered her voice,

but her tone didn't soften. "This is an unexpected setback, but we're nearing the end of the year when people need tax write-offs."

True, but doubts swirled in Paige's mind. She wasn't good at wooing donors. She was too honest, too direct, and didn't play games. Much to Amanda's dismay. "Raising the initial amount took longer than anyone expected."

"Yet, we raised it. Your spiel swayed many influential people."

Paige stiffened. "It wasn't a spiel. The hospital needs a cancer center."

Dollar signs shone in Amanda's eyes. "We don't want to lose patients to other hospitals."

"We want to provide the best care possible to cancer patients," Paige said a beat later.

Amanda's priority was increasing hospital profits. Paige understood that. But the project meant more than profits to her. She hated asking for money, but she'd exhausted every avenue to raise the funds to build a dedicated facility with a top-notch multidisciplinary team of caregivers. The center would handle both outpatients and inpatients. The specially designed rooms and waiting areas would provide cancer patients and their families with the spaces they deserved. Thinking about the possibilities for clinical research and clinical studies excited her.

A nurse who Paige didn't recognize exited one room and went into another.

Paige waited for the door to close before turning her attention on Amanda. "What do you need from me?"

"You sold people on this center before. I need you to do it again."

O-kay. Not surprising. Paige had found herself in a different role than what she was familiar with while seeking donations. But for whatever reason, she'd had better luck convincing people than others who'd tried before her.

"When?" she asked.

"Tomorrow."

Paige blew out a breath. "That soon?"

Amanda nodded once.

Sunday was Paige's day off—her only day this week—but the center was too important to put off. The hospital currently had a cancer care unit for inpatients, but that couldn't compare to what the center would provide.

"Where do I need to be and when?" she asked.

"Henry Davenport is sponsoring a party here at the children's hospital tomorrow afternoon at four."

Henry had donated the wing that housed the children's hospital, but a caution light blared in Paige's brain. "Henry made a sizeable donation to the cancer center already. His current pet project is a new NICU."

"It won't hurt to ask him."

That was true. If Henry couldn't donate, he might be able to tell her who to approach. He was friends with the most influential and wealthy individuals in the area. "I'll speak to him and whoever else is there."

"I'll be there, too, so I can provide backup, but I'm a stuffy administrator. Your enthusiasm for this project will sell them on the cancer center."

Paige stood taller. Compliments from Amanda were rare. "Thank you."

"Before I forget, Henry asked everyone to dress Christmassy," Amanda said.

Paige thought of her ugly sweater, holiday-patterned leggings, and Christmas jewelry. Items she'd been too busy to pull down from the bin from the top of her closet. "Not a problem."

"You look exhausted. Go home and sleep," Amanda ordered. "You've put in your time as an intern and resident. Reap the benefits now."

Paige nearly snorted. Yeah, those years had been challenging, but she didn't have set hours each day now. She never knew what might happen or how long she might work.

But Amanda was right about one thing. Paige was finished for the night. She could go home. Her plans, however, had changed. She would skip watching any movies and go to bed instead. She wanted to be bright-eyed and well-rested before she found a non-tacky way to ask Henry for another donation.

* * *

On Sunday at five o'clock, Paige crossed the skybridge from the main hospital to the children's wing. She'd planned to arrive earlier, but rounds had taken longer than she expected. At least her ugly reindeer sweater with a light-up red nose, snowmen-patterned leggings, and antler headband had amused her adult patients. Now to see what the younger patients thought…

And Henry Davenport.

She wanted him to like her Christmas outfit. That might soften him up a bit when she asked for money.

As she made her way to the floor where the event was being held, Paige mentally rehearsed what she wanted to say about needing additional funding. Fundraising wasn't something that came naturally to her. To be honest, she hated it, but her dream of a new cancer center had pushed her out of her comfort zone. Now, she had to do that again. Only a few more times, Paige hoped. But she wanted to be careful because this wasn't a charity gala where people expected to be asked for donations.

As she approached the party, the scents of vanilla, cinnamon, and peppermint lingered in the hallway. She inhaled, relishing the smells. With each step, the strains of a cheery Christmas tune grew louder, but something else rose above the music—laughter.

Young, loud, joyful.

The best sound ever.

Paige's entire body felt as if it were smiling. She quickened her pace. When she reached the entrance, she stopped, freezing in place as if her shoes had become encased in cement.

She couldn't move—didn't want to move. Instead, she stared in awe at the whimsical winter wonderland in front of her.

Breathtaking.

Paige blinked, half expecting the sight to disappear, but the enchanted party room was still there.

Intricate snowflakes hung from the ceiling. Fairy lights twinkled on artificial trees, glowed around the windows, and lit up the walls. Fake snowmen had been accessorized, but an entire snow family waited to be decorated with scarves, hats, and other items.

The best part, though?

The children's smiling, bright faces.

Some wore masks over their mouths and noses, but their eyes twinkled with excitement. The magic of Christmas was alive and well.

Paige forced herself to move. The room wasn't crowded, and she assumed that was on purpose so patients and their families could rotate in and out without becoming too overwhelmed or tired. She'd enjoyed her pediatrics rotation, but she'd preferred working with adults. Still, she was called in occasionally to give her opinion on certain patients as she had last night.

Across the room, Henry Davenport kneeled in front of a child who appeared captivated by the billionaire's nutcracker tie. That wasn't the only holiday attire Henry wore. His suit was Christmas-themed, too. His jacket was a candy cane-patterned fabric with red lapels. Holly was embroidered down the sides of his pants. Henry looked more like a boss elf from the North Pole than one of the country's leading philanthropists.

"Ho, ho, ho." Santa sat on an oversized chair. He made a convincing Kris Kringle with his fancy suit, white beard that looked almost real, wire-rimmed glasses, shiny boots, a hat, and padding around his middle. "Come over here, and tell Santa what you'd like for Christmas."

Wait. Paige did a double take. He appeared to be looking at her.

She glanced around. No one else was nearby. She pointed at herself. "Me?"

Santa nodded. "More kids will be here soon. Now's your chance to visit with me before a line forms."

Heat rushed up her neck. "Thanks, but I'm a little old."

"More than one parent has told Santa what they wanted for Christmas."

A healthy child.

People took health for granted until they or a

loved one became sick and their lives changed.

"No one is too old to talk to me." He spoke as if he was trying to deepen his voice, but she supposed Santa would be more baritone or bass than tenor.

She shrugged. When she'd been younger, seeing Santa had been one of her favorite traditions, but that had been years—decades—ago.

"Isn't there something *you* want?" he asked.

Feeling surprisingly uncertain, Paige nodded.

"I thought so." Santa adjusted his glasses. The beard hid most of his lower face, but his cheeks weren't rosy. Still, hazel eyes twinkled.

His eyes.

She took a closer look. Something about them seemed familiar. The color or shape. Maybe he was a friend of Henry's or a staff member at the hospital.

"Christmas is a magical time, perfect for making wishes and asking for miracles," Santa continued. "So let's hear what you hope to find under the tree this year."

She pushed aside her misgivings.

"Okay." Her Christmas wish was a big one and might require a miracle when all was said and done. "But don't say I didn't warn you."

"I'm up for the challenge," he countered.

At least the guy hadn't said he'd find out using his magical crystal snow globe. She had to give it to Henry. This Santa wasn't bad. Though, she wasn't sitting on his lap.

Santa padded the armrest as if reading her mind. "There's space right here."

Mindful of her hips where she carried any extra weight, Paige sat, careful to keep her distance from Santa. Still, her muscles tensed, no doubt stressed over how to raise the money. She blew out a breath, but that didn't help her relax.

Jingling bells caught her attention.

Across the room, Henry led two children in a rousing rendition of "Jingle Bells."

So cute. Paige smiled. A part of her wanted to sing along. The spirit of Christmas must be contagious, and she hoped each person here today caught it.

"You like kids," Santa said.

"I do." She watched the trio sing another verse. "Someday I want a husband, kids, dog, cat, and a house with a fenced yard. That's how I envision my happily ever after."

Oops. Had she said that aloud? Based on Santa's grin, she must have.

"Someday or now?"

"Someday, so you don't need to worry about fitting all that in your sleigh this time."

Paige, however, wouldn't say no to meeting her future spouse, but a relationship would be easier after the cancer center was underway. And she doubted Santa played matchmaker.

"What do you want this year?" he asked.

"I want…need…"

Henry hugged each of the kids who had been singing with him. Everyone was so happy. She couldn't bring herself to say the amount.

This party was for the children and their families. It wasn't the right time to approach Henry for a donation. Even if that meant dealing with Amanda's wrath, Paige would find a more appropriate time to reach out to the philanthropist.

"If you can't tell Santa, who can you tell?" His tone was lighthearted and teasing.

Except he wasn't Santa. He was a random guy in a red suit. But him being a stranger was even better. Telling him the amount might make saying it to Henry or someone else easier.

Worth a try.

"Twenty-five million dollars," she whispered.

Santa didn't gasp. He didn't flinch or blink. His expression didn't change one bit. Maybe he went to Santa school, where he learned how not to react when a kid asked for a live tiger in her stocking or a magic wand that would turn his teachers into toads or a cure for cancer. Twenty-five million dollars was in the realm of unrealistic gifts.

"It's not something you can do anything about, so I don't expect to find that under my Christmas tree." Even if Santa Claus was real, that amount would be way over his gift limit. "But I'll gladly take a candy cane."

"That I can do." Smiling, Santa reached over the

other armrest. When he raised his hand, he held a candy cane tied with a red satin ribbon. "May I ask why that amount?"

Paige glanced around to see if anyone was nearby. Everyone had joined in more caroling so no one was paying attention to her and Santa. She wasn't trying to be secretive, but she didn't want Henry to hear. Not today.

"A project—something I'm passionate about—is short on funding. Twenty-five-million-dollars short." Saying the amount again was easier. "But as you said, Christmas is a magical time. With a sprinkle of elf pixie dust, everything will work out."

Stop talking. You're rambling.

Not surprising because she did better as Dr. Regis wearing her white coat than as Paige in a Christmas outfit. But she believed her wish would come true. Somehow. Some way.

"It will." Santa handed her the candy cane. "Merry Christmas."

She took it from him. "Merry Christmas, Santa."

As more people entered the party, she headed toward Amanda. Henry stepped in front of Paige, blocking her path.

"Dr. Regis." He greeted her with a wide grin. The man was as handsome as he was charming. "So happy you could join our holiday soiree."

"You've outdone yourself."

"Anything for the kids, but the credit goes to the

event planner I hired." He motioned to Paige's sweater. "Thanks for dressing up."

"I heard it was mandatory."

"Optional, but highly recommended." He glanced toward Santa, who was speaking with a young girl in a wheelchair. "Did you tell Santa you wanted twenty-five million dollars for Christmas?"

Paige's shoulders sagged. "Amanda spoke to you about it."

Henry nodded. "Probably because you didn't arrive on time."

"Rounds."

"Which is what I told her," he said to Paige's surprise.

"How did you know that?" she asked.

"I remember how diligent you were the times Wes was in the hospital."

Whenever Wes Lockhart, a patient of hers, had been hospitalized, Henry and Blaise Mortenson alternated staying overnight. During the day, other men took shifts, too. Not once during any of Wes's stays had Paige found him alone, which told her how deep his bonds of friendship went.

"Thank you." That was the easiest thing for her to say even if all she'd been doing was her job. "How is Wes doing these days?"

Henry laughed, a deep bellowing sound.

"What's so funny?" she asked.

His eyes lit with a hint of mischief. "You just

spoke to him."

Huh? And then it hit her. The familiar hazel eyes she couldn't quite place. Her stomach flip-flopped. She swallowed around the lump in her throat. "Wes is Santa?"

Henry nodded. "I thought he'd be a good one, and he must be if you didn't recognize him."

Wes was so good at playing the role she'd asked him for twenty-five million dollars.

Ugh.

He'd been her patient during the initial fundraising efforts. Yes, he had billions and a charity foundation. But Paige had seen him at his lowest point. He had such a strong personality and drive, but the weight of his diagnosis had crippled him. After he went into remission, he'd had two follow-up visits with her before being referred to his primary care physician, who saw Wes every three to four months.

Paige hated that she hadn't recognized him. He'd deepened his voice to not sound like his normal self. The hat and beard hid much of his face.

"He never broke character," she said.

Henry beamed. "That's part of the Santa creed."

"There's a creed?"

"If not, there should be." He lowered his voice. "This party was my last charitable donation for the year. My investment guru and so-called friend, Brett Matthews, has cut me off from giving more until the new year. If you haven't raised the funds by then, please call me."

"Thank you." Paige straightened, grateful for Henry's generosity. "I will, but I hope to have the money before then."

"Good luck."

She half laughed. "I need it."

"You'll do fine." Henry motioned to Santa—Wes—who spoke to a young boy who couldn't stop giggling. "Talk to Wes after the party. He hasn't been back to the hospital for a while."

"There's been no reason for him to visit." She could spout off the five-year survival rate for Hodgkin's lymphoma patients and other statistics, but numbers didn't tell a patient's story. Each case was unique. Wes had experienced unexpected setbacks and complications, but he'd gone into remission. Something she wished would happen with all her patients. "My goal is for him not to return."

"You succeeded."

"We did." She might be an oncologist, but she was only one part of a larger team of caregivers, each who worked in tandem to help patients like Wes. "But if he has to be here, this party is the way to do it."

Henry grinned proudly. "I agree."

A little girl trying to wrap a scarf around a snowman's neck stomped her slipper-covered foot. She pouted. "Mr. Henry, it's not working right."

"Duty calls." Henry gave a mock bow. "It's a pleasure to see you again. Enjoy the party, Dr. Regis."

With that, he hurried over to help accessorize the snowman.

Someone tugged on her arm.

A child—around six or seven—had a bandage wrapped around his head. He pulled at her sweater. "I like Rudolph's red nose."

"Me, too."

"Are you a mommy?" he asked.

"I work at the hospital." Paige didn't see any adults hovering nearby. She kneeled to bring herself to his eye level. "Is there something you need?"

Hope filled the boy's eyes. "Do you want to color with me?"

Paige didn't know if he was here alone or what, but that didn't matter. She grinned. "I'd love to color."

"I'm Dalton."

"It's nice to meet you," she said. "I'm Paige."

Smiling, he grabbed her hand. "I'll take you to the coloring station."

"Lead the way." She couldn't think of a better activity to do while she waited for Wes.

Chapter Three

After the party, Wes changed into jeans and a sweater in the men's room. He expected the hours spent being charming and ho-ho-ho-ing to wear him out, but he felt exhilarated, ready for...more. That told him one thing.

Henry was correct.

Wes placed the Santa suit and boots into the garment bag and zipped it up.

No matter how much he wanted to remain detached, he was missing out by keeping his distance from those his foundation helped. As Henry had said, people needed to know others cared, but Wes needed something also, something he hadn't realized until playing Santa.

He needed the connection.

Not an email or a letter full of gratitude, but the face-to-face connection with another human being. Sure, he had lots of interactions at work. His company had over two thousand employees, and he made himself visible there. But this…

This was different.

Something else he hadn't understood until tonight.

Washing his hands, Wes stared at his reflection in the mirror above the sink.

"What do you want for Christmas?" he asked himself.

He'd quadrupled the profits of his family's company, amassing money and awards and fame. He'd found a second family composed of friends who understood the craziness such success brought. He'd survived lymphoma. At thirty-five, he'd accomplished so much.

But it wasn't enough.

People wanted to be him, which he didn't understand.

Most of them saw the outer Weston E. Lockhart IV. Few looked beyond his net worth to the man underneath. One who was unsettled and lonely. Who was more than a little worried and uncertain about what might come next.

He dried his hands.

What did Wes want for Christmas?

He wanted to feel this happy and content every

day.

Tonight showed him signing a check was nowhere near as fulfilling as listening to a child's Christmas wish or seeing a smile brighten their face or hearing their laughter. As each clutched their present from Santa, he'd felt like the most important person in the world—their world. Despite their illnesses, they grinned and said thank you, filling him with unfamiliar contentment.

He wanted more of that.

His plan for the holidays had been to make a difference in people's lives by donating money. The foundation still could do that, but *he* would get more involved. He could help not only strangers, but also those who had made a difference in his life.

Starting with Dr. Paige Regis.

Thinking about her brought a rush of warmth. Wes hadn't expected to see her at the party, let alone dressed up like an advertisement for Christmas with her caramel hair worn loose and her eyes full of wonder. Her uncertainty about talking to Santa was so unlike the focused, cancer-fighting warrior he'd depended upon during his treatments.

Different, but appealing on a whole other level.

Dr. Regis was the definition of serious. Wes had appreciated her dedication as she guided him through the toughest fight of his life. He would be eternally grateful for her care, but tonight, he saw there was so much more to her than a talented medical professional.

That intrigued him.

Who was he kidding?

This new side of her captivated Wes—made him want to learn more about her, which surprised him.

Not that he would do anything about that. But he could do something else.

Twenty-five million dollars.

She'd shared with Santa what she wanted this year. It wasn't a gift for herself because the cancer center would benefit others. People who'd been sick like him and Zeke. Some would get a second chance like Wes. Others might find more comfort in their final days.

Yes, Wes would make her Christmas wish come true.

With a plan in mind, he returned to the party room and handed over the garment bag to Henry. "Thanks for the loan."

"How was playing Santa?"

"You were right." Wes didn't hesitate answering. "I should be more involved with helping others. Giving money is one thing, but this felt…right."

Henry's smile spread. "As I said, some people don't know what they need."

"You did." People, including Rachael Reese who planned the event, packed up items. None of the hospital staff were there. That was a bummer. "Have you seen Dr. Regis?"

"She was here a few minutes ago."

"She isn't now." Wes hadn't thought she might leave right away. "I'll call her office on Monday."

"About the twenty-five million?"

He nodded. "That's what she mentioned to Santa. I'm happy to do that for her."

"Excellent, but how will you make the donation personal?"

"What do you mean?" Wes asked.

"Most sizeable donations are sent by a check or bank transfer."

"Sadie will figure out the logistics."

"You just told me you wanted to be personally involved."

Wes had. "But money is what Dr. Regis wants."

"Maybe there's something else she needs. Something for herself."

Someday I want a husband, kids, dog, cat, and a house with a fenced yard. That's how I envision my happily ever after.

Nope. That was beyond Wes. Besides, she hadn't wanted that this year.

And then he had an idea. "She likes candy canes."

Henry rolled his eyes. "A grand gesture isn't necessary, but you need to do something more than give her sweets."

Wes had zero ideas that didn't involve giving her money. "This is hard."

"The effort makes it more special."

A minute passed. Maybe two.

Henry straightened. "Invite Dr. Regis to the dinner in Hood Hamlet on Saturday."

Hood Hamlet was located on Mount Hood, approximately sixty miles from Portland. The quaint alpine-inspired small town was where he spent most weekends. The place was always charming but shined brightest during the holidays. The Christmas Magic in Hood Hamlet celebration began in the morning and culminated with a dinner and silent auction to benefit Oregon Mountain Search and Rescue and the Hood Hamlet Fire and Rescue's Christmas Toy Drive. The fun festivities benefited two good causes.

Thinking about showing Dr. Regis the town sent a thrill shooting through Wes. Until he remembered. "Why would I do that? I'm taking a break from dating."

Henry tsked. "Who said anything about a date? Dr. Regis can be your plus-one."

That might work, except… "I might not go."

"You purchased two tables of eight. We'll all be there. Adam and Cambria, Blaise and Hadley, Brett and Laurel, Dash and Raina, Kieran and Selah, Mason and Rachael, me and a beautiful woman who will think she won the lottery being my date. Of course you're going, and you're bringing a guest." Henry emphasized the last word. "Not a date."

"The foundation—"

"Give your staff the night off. It's time you represent the foundation yourself."

Emotion clogged Wes's throat.

"I understood why you didn't want to attend anything when you were feeling so bad. Plus all the germs, but now…" Henry shook his head. "You are *healthy*, Wes. You have nothing to prove to anyone. Stop hiding as if something's still wrong with you."

Wes raised his chin. "I'm not hiding."

"Good, because the dinner is the perfect place for Dr. Regis to make the connections she needs. Several, if not all of us, met her during your treatments and hospital stays, so this will be a great time to reintroduce her to everybody."

Wait. Had Wes missed something? With Henry, anything was possible. "Why do I need to reintroduce Dr. Regis to people?"

"Remember when I donated this hospital wing?" Henry's voice was louder than before. Two of the catering staff glanced over.

Wes ignored them. "Yes, and you named it after your parents."

"This hospital is the one thing I've done in my life that might have made my mom and dad proud." Henry's sad tone matched the regret in his gaze. His parents had loved him, but both had wanted him to do more with his life than be a trust-fund baby. "But it wasn't a single donation like I thought it would be. Changes to the plans—some necessary and not extravagant—cost more."

"You paid for the overruns."

"I was the sole benefactor for the project. I was happy to pay for whatever they needed," Henry explained. "But the cancer center's budget comes from multiple sources. That's why Dr. Regis needs to become familiar with those in our circle. That way, she'll have additional people to go to when more money is needed."

When, not if.

The word wasn't lost on Wes. "No one ever approached me for a donation to the cancer center."

"You were in the middle of treatments." Henry's tone was softer now. Compassionate. "Asking you for money would have been tacky and inappropriate."

Wes shrugged. Dr. Regis hadn't asked him for a donation this time, either. She'd told a fake Santa what she needed. If she hadn't, Wes wouldn't know about it. "Did you donate to the cancer center?"

"Yes, and I'd give more now, but Brett has cut me off from additional charitable giving until January. This party and the presents for the patients was my last hurrah for the year. Other than the toy I'll bring to the dinner on Saturday night."

Wes laughed. Henry had been Brett's first investment client, but their lifelong friendship was…complicated. "Giving away too much money again?"

"I have more than I could spend in several lifetimes, but you know Brett. He worries too much about my ability to maintain my lifestyle in the future."

"That's what a friend and financial advisor should do."

"He's annoying." Henry sighed. "Can you believe Brett laughed when I told him I see myself as a modern-day Robin Hood?"

"Yes." But no matter Brett's concerns, Henry was the most generous person Wes knew. Given their friend group, that was saying something. "You realize you're stealing from yourself."

"Semantics. The gesture is the same. Or will be again, once the new year arrives." Henry tilted his head, motioning to his right. "Dr. Regis is back. Now's your chance to make a donation and invite her to the dinner."

Butterflies set flight in Wes's stomach. An unexpected reaction because talking with Dr. Regis was business. Nothing else. "Okay."

"Let me know what she says about both," Henry whispered in a conspiratorial tone. "I'm off to Brett and Laurel's house. I want to see Noelle before she goes to bed."

Henry was Noelle's godfather, and he adored the little girl. On his way out, he said something to Dr. Regis.

She laughed.

The melodic sound smacked into Wes like a sucker punch.

The butterflies in his stomach quadrupled or

maybe they doubled in size or turned into helicopters. The reaction surprised him. When he'd been her patient, he'd noticed she was attractive. He had been sick, but he was still a man. He also might have had a crush—albeit a slight one—when she'd been so dedicated and focused on helping him kick the cancer to the curb. Something she'd done like a real-life superhero minus the cape.

But he'd never analyzed or thought much about her looks. Now, he couldn't stop noticing everything about her.

How when she laughed, her nose crinkled at the top. That her blue eyes shone bright like precious gemstones. The way her wide smile lit up her heart-shaped face with a radiant glow. And her full, pink lips…

He blinked.

What was he doing? What was he thinking?

Dr. Regis was a professional. She'd saved his life. Sure, attractive no longer seemed the right adjective to describe her, but she deserved better than him leering.

As she headed his way, his muscles twitched.

What was wrong with him? He'd known Dr. Regis for over two years. She'd seen him at his worst. The realization immediately humbled him.

Embarrassed him.

Even if Wes wanted to date—which he didn't— he wouldn't want to go out with someone who knew his weaknesses, had watched him fall apart more than once, and had seen him sob.

Her smile wavered, but only for a second. "You're still here."

"So are you." Wes fought the urge to grimace. That wasn't the most eloquent response. At least he hadn't called her dude as Dash often did. "I thought you left."

"A patient's parents couldn't be here today," she explained. "I went to his room with him for a few minutes."

He respected how she showed the same kindness and compassion to people whether or not they were her patients. "Was that the little boy you were coloring with?"

Great, now Wes sounded like he was stalking her. He should forget wanting to do more and just send a check before he made a bigger fool out of himself.

"Yes, his name is Dalton. He's very sweet," she said. "Artistic, too. His picture came out nicer than mine."

"He paid a visit to Santa." Dalton had told Santa the only thing he wanted was to have his family together for Christmas, but that request wasn't to be shared with anyone, including Dr. Regis.

"I bet he mentioned his family to you," she said.

Not only intelligent, but perceptive. Wes nodded.

"He misses them," she continued. "But Christmas is still seventeen days away. Lots can happen between now and then."

Wes wondered if she was only talking about Dalton. "Are you spending the holidays with your family?"

"No. I'm on call this year."

"Sorry."

"Don't be," she replied quickly. "It's part of the job. I'll still have a nice holiday."

Wes glanced at her ring finger. Bare. That made him curious. "With your boyfriend?"

"No boyfriend." She laughed, more of a nervous giggle than amusement over his question. "I suppose that's the first step to having a husband, so maybe I should have asked Santa for one of those."

"I can help you out."

Her eyes widened, and her mouth dropped open, but no words came out.

He realized what he'd said.

"I meant with the other thing you wanted. Not a boyfriend. A donation." Just shoot him now because he appeared hopeless where Dr. Regis was concerned. "I want to help you with the cancer center."

"Wonderful, while having a boyfriend might be nice, the cancer center is my priority, so thank you." Excitement filled her eyes. "What do you have in mind?"

People were still cleaning up. Rachael Reese watched him closely. She would report back to Mason, who would ask about what his wife mentioned on their group chat, and then everyone would have questions. That had happened to Blaise when he first met Hadley and when Dash went out with Raina. The same thing occurred with Adam, Kieran, and Mason and their respective girlfriends-now wives.

No, thanks.

"Do you have time to grab a coffee?" That would give them a place to talk with no one trying to eavesdrop. Not that Rachael was. Yet. "I remember a place not too far away."

"I'm free," Paige said. "There's a coffee shop half a block from here that's open late."

"Sounds great. Ready to go?"

She nodded. "I just need to grab my purse on our way out."

Ten minutes later, Wes sat across from her at a small round table tucked in a back corner. He sipped his Americano.

"I would have taken you for the caramel macchiato type." He eyed her mug, which was topped with whipped cream, chocolate sprinkles, and a candy cane. "Not peppermint hot chocolate."

"It's a Christmas drink. Not as traditional as eggnog, but a close second."

She took a sip. When she lowered her mug from her mouth, a dollop of whipped cream stuck to her upper lip.

Wes shouldn't be staring or wishing he could help her with it. He tried to look away, but he couldn't.

Fighting the urge to wipe it off, he handed her a napkin. "You have whipped cream on your mouth."

"That always happens with these drinks." She patted her face with the napkin. "But it's worth it."

Glad she thought so. Wes never imagined himself envying a napkin, especially when he wasn't interested in dating. Since Annabelle, he'd been on one date set up by a matchmaker—Blaise Mortenson's misguided attempt to win the last-single-man-standing bet. Wes had done his duty as a friend and gone out with a woman, but his heart hadn't been in it. He didn't want—couldn't have—anyone in his life. Not like that.

"Nice place," he said.

"I come here a lot."

The cozy setting with low lighting and soft instrumental versions of Christmas carols playing would be perfect for a date. "After work?"

"All the time. My condo is around the corner."

"I had no idea you lived this close." And then it hit him. Why would he? Wes only knew what was written on the oncology practice's website's bio. He'd been focused on himself at his appointments. He'd never thought to ask about her. "Do you walk to the hospital?"

She nodded. "It's faster than driving because of parking."

"That would be convenient."

"For me, yes. I'm guessing you work as much at

home as you do at your office."

"I used to," he admitted. "I've been working less since…"

Wes sipped his coffee. He hadn't wanted to bring up the cancer. She'd probably had enough of that.

"I'm happy to hear you're finding more balance," she said. "It's something many people struggle with."

"You?"

Her mouth slanted. "More than I care to admit."

"And living this close…"

"As you said, convenient, but it has drawbacks, too."

He set his drink on the table. "The center will bring more work."

"At the beginning, yes. There are times I feel I'm wearing multiple hats besides my doctor one, but once we are fully staffed, my involvement in the actual project will lessen."

Was that why she talked about "someday" for the other things she wanted? That would make sense, though it was none of his business. But something else was. "So let's discuss your cancer center, Dr. Regis."

"Please, call me Paige."

"Paige." Wes liked how the name sounded. "I want to donate twenty-five million dollars."

Her lips parted. "You… Really? Just like that?"

Her dumbfounded expression was cute. "I need to run this by my foundation, but yes. Just like that."

"I…" Her eyes gleamed. "Thank you. There's so much more I should say, but my brain isn't functioning at the moment."

Wes understood because he was having trouble, too. He wanted to celebrate with a hug, but he ignored the urge. "I'd also like to do something else."

"Twenty-five million is plenty." The words shot out. Her jaw tensed. "I know I'm supposed to say I'll graciously accept whatever you want to do, but fundraising is hard for me. I prefer working for what I want, not having to ask someone for it."

He respected her work ethic. "With the center, you don't have a choice."

She nodded. "But I don't want you to feel obligated—"

"I don't," he said before she could finish. This was more about her than his being sick. "The cancer center will fulfill a need. That's why I'm donating."

"Okay, thanks."

"The center may need more donations if the plans change or you need to implement a new technology. Assets aren't always liquid, which could stop me or Henry from helping. That's why I want you to get to know friends of mine. You met them briefly when I was having treatments, but I want to reintroduce you. Not at the hospital though."

"Okay. Wow." Her smile reached her eyes. "That sounds wonderful. Tell me when."

"Saturday. There's a fundraising dinner in Hood

Hamlet. Everyone will be there."

She checked her phone. "I'm not on call, so all I need to know is the time and location."

"Great."

Paige nodded. "I've heard Hood Hamlet is a charming small town."

"I own a house there." That gave Wes an idea. "You should drive up in the morning and make a day of it. I can show you around. The dinner is only one part of the Christmas Magic in Hood Hamlet celebration. There's caroling, horse-drawn sleigh rides, cookie decorating, a craft bazaar, chocolate tasting, and a snow-sculpture contest."

"Sounds like something from a Christmas movie."

"That's exactly what it is."

"Then I'll enjoy it because I'm addicted to a certain cable channel during the holidays."

"You'll love Hood Hamlet."

"I can't wait." She sounded breathless, but she had every right to be tonight. "Twenty-five million dollars, an intro to the movers and shakers in the Silicon Forest, and a day exploring a small-town holiday celebration. Are you really Santa Claus in disguise, pretending to be a billionaire?"

That made him laugh. "I'm just Wes. The suit belongs to Henry. But I enjoyed playing Kris Kringle so much, I might have to be a secret Santa this year."

"Too late," she quipped. "You're already my not-so-secret Santa. But I'm sure no one will complain if you want to keep it up."

He laughed.

So did she.

Then they both sipped their drinks.

Wes hadn't felt so lighthearted in... He couldn't remember the last time. He lowered his coffee and unlocked his phone before handing it to her. "Before I forget, give me your number."

She tapped on the screen. A second later a beep sounded from her purse. "Now we have each other's contact info."

"Thanks." He placed his cell phone in his pocket. "I'll speak with the head of my foundation to find out how we proceed with the donation, and then I'll be in touch about that and Hood Hamlet."

"Perfect," she said.

Wes had the feeling everything, including this coming weekend, would be perfect. And he couldn't wait.

Chapter Four

*P*erfect.

The word described how Paige felt about hearing Wes would be in touch with her, but it also described what sitting with him in her favorite coffee shop felt like. The night couldn't get any better. She wiggled her toes.

The twenty-five-million-dollar donation would make her Christmas wish come true. His wanting her to get to know his affluent friends could help the cancer center in the future. And having the undivided attention of a hot billionaire tonight didn't suck.

This wasn't a date, but she imagined the same scenario happening in one of the holiday movies she loved to watch. Wes could easily be a leading man with his thick, dark hair, classically handsome features, expressive hazel eyes, and an easy smile. His gray peacoat hung off the back of his chair. His V-neck black sweater hugged his chest and arms, showing off a fit physique.

Seeing Wes looking so healthy and seemingly happy sent warmth and pride flowing through Paige. Tonight was a far cry from where he'd been at the crux of his illness, and the reason she loved her job. No, she couldn't help all patients, even though she did everything she could, but those like Wes, who went into remission, helped her deal with the bad stuff.

He set his glass on the table before glancing around.

Was it time to say goodbye?

Wes knew how to contact her, but Paige wasn't ready for the night to end. She wanted to know more about his life post-cancer.

She glanced into her cup. "I still have some hot cocoa left. If you have to be somewhere, go ahead and take off. I want to finish my drink before I leave."

"I can stay." He leaned back in his chair. "I haven't drunk all of mine and don't want it to go to waste."

She nearly laughed. Wes could buy his own coffee shop without a second thought, but he wanted to drink the last drop of his Americano. Maybe that was why he'd amassed so much wealth. He didn't waste money.

"So what have you been up to?" she asked.

He stretched out his legs. "I was just about to ask how you spend your time when you're not working."

"I'll start because my life is the definition of boring, so it won't take me long," she admitted. "My days don't vary. Everything revolves around work. When I get home, I eat. I might watch television and read, but there are times I'm too tired and fall into bed. I occasionally go out with a group of friends, but most of them are now in relationships or married. It can be difficult being the odd person out, so I try not to put myself into that situation too often."

Pathetic, but true.

"I have little free time outside of the hospital, and I tend toward being a homebody. As I said, boring," she added.

Wes leaned forward. "Having a routine isn't boring. It's better than filling every minute with things you don't really enjoy doing."

She raised a brow. "Speaking from experience?"

"Maybe." Humor lit his eyes. "Let's just say, some positives came out of the cancer. I rethought what I was doing."

"That happens more than you'd think." She took a sip. "Second chances and all."

A thoughtful expression crossed his face before he nodded. "I understand about being single when everyone else is part of a couple. Last year, my friend Brett got married. He was the only one of our friends who was. But now, four more have said 'I do.' Another has a girlfriend. Henry and I are the only unattached ones now."

The two were flat-out catches as far as she could tell. "Both of you could remedy your relationship status if you wanted to."

Wes smiled. "I suppose we could, but I don't want to. Henry feels the same way."

Paige remembered when Wes's girlfriend had stopped coming to his appointments, and his friends stepped in to support him. He'd never said a word to her, but rumors about the socialite dumping him over his illness had been everywhere.

"So that's why you need a plus-one for the dinner," Paige teased.

"Guilty." A beat later, he shook his head. "To be honest, I wasn't sure I was going until tonight. I haven't been to any events for a while."

That surprised her. From what she'd heard, Wes had been a mainstay at galas and parties but maybe he'd stopped attending after his diagnosis. She would have thought he'd returned to the same social activities since he was better. "I'm honored, then."

"You should be," he deadpanned. "Seriously, Saturday will be good for both of us."

"It will."

Before she met Wes Lockhart, his reputation had preceded him. Her partners at the practice had raised concerns about his strong ego and personality to the point Paige worried how he would be as a patient. But the man who arrived for his first office visit had been the opposite of a brash, corporate raider who fired employees at the companies he took over.

Something clattered against the floor behind the counter.

The sound jolted Paige. She'd forgotten they weren't alone in the coffee shop.

"I told you about me." What little there was to tell, but he didn't know that. "It's your turn."

Wes fiddled with the edge of a small napkin. "Work is still the biggest part of my life, but I've cut back my hours."

She remembered when he'd told her his daily schedule. "Does that mean you've gone from a hundred twenty-plus hours a week to what, eighty or ninety?"

Wes laughed. "I didn't realize you knew me that well."

Paige shrugged, but the last thing she felt was indifferent. His workload had concerned her when he was sick because she'd known he wouldn't be able to keep up that pace during his treatments. "You get to know someone after two years."

Though she had a feeling he couldn't say the same thing about her. Which was on purpose.

"I've been trying to find a better balance," he admitted.

One of his biggest fears had been what effect his

cancer would have on his company, W.E. Lockhart Inc., aka WEL. But both had survived, and he appeared to be thriving. She hoped his company was, too.

Paige respected Wes, but it had nothing to do with his success or wealth. At his weakest physically, he'd shown admirable strength and determination. Now he was taking care of himself, which made her proud.

"I don't want work to be my life," he added.

"I'm so happy to hear that." Paige worked even when she planned to be off. But one of these days, she would have the life and schedule she wanted. "Maybe you can give me pointers on how to do that."

He flashed her a lopsided grin. "Isn't the doctor supposed to know best?"

"We're still human."

"*No, you're* not." His voice was firm, and she couldn't tell whether or not he was kidding. "You keep your cape and superpowers hidden, but you have them and use them."

If he wanted to see her as a caped cancer crusader, who was Paige to argue with that? She feigned outrage. "Who told you?"

That made him laugh. Her, too.

Paige had no idea how long she and Wes talked, but she enjoyed every minute. When she raised her cup to take a sip, no hot cocoa remained, that didn't stop their conversation that never dragged. Topics bounced from football—both of them rooted for Seattle—to the Nutcracker ballet—they disagreed over whether it needed to be seen more than once.

A barista approached the table. He wore a black apron over his long-sleeved T-shirt and jeans. "We're closing in a few minutes. If you want anything to go, please order it now."

As the guy returned to the counter, Paige pulled out her phone. It was almost ten. "I lost track of the time."

"Me, too. I had no idea they were about to close." Wes scooted back in his chair. "Ready?"

Nodding, she stood, put on her coat, and exited the coffee shop. As he shrugged on his jacket, he followed her.

Outside an older man with a small white dog wearing a pink sweater passed by them. A few cars were on the road, but not as many as earlier.

The temperature had dropped, too. Her breath hung on the air. "Thanks for the drink. This was nice."

"It was." Wes put on his gloves. "I'll walk you home."

"It isn't far." She left her mittens in her pocket to emphasize how close she lived.

"Humor me."

Two words that could be taken a different way, but his tone was concerned, not condescending.

Paige knew the risks of living in the city. If she

felt unsafe, she didn't walk home alone, but Wes didn't know that about her. Not really. He'd only interacted with her as his doctor until tonight. "Okay, I'll humor you. It's to the left."

She headed in that direction.

As he fell in step beside her, his smile warmed her insides, reaffirming she'd done the right thing.

"Thank you," he said.

She zipped up her jacket to keep from getting chilled. "That should be my line after everything you've done or are doing for the cancer center and me."

"What you did when I was sick trumps everything, including the donation."

Paige probably shouldn't ask, but she wanted to know. "Is that why you're donating?"

"Yes and no," Wes admitted. "You did so much for me, I want to help you. But others need the cancer center."

"I appreciate your honesty." Wishing she'd pulled out her gloves, she shoved her hands into her pockets. "I hope you know a payback isn't required."

"I know. But…"

The way his voice trailed off piqued her curiosity. "What?"

"With the cancer in remission, I've been given a second chance." His earnest tone tugged at her heart. "I want to make the most of it."

"Is that how you ended up being Santa tonight?"

"Henry needed help. He thought this was a good start."

"A great one. I can't wait to see what you do next."

"Really?" He spoke louder, like an excited kid.

Talk about adorable. Which was a word she had never associated with Wes Lockhart before.

"Really," Paige repeated. "After everything you've been through, this new direction is inspiring. I'm so happy you want to live life to the fullest and help others."

His grin lit up his face. "That means a lot."

She stopped in front of her building's entrance. "This is me."

He appeared to study each of the four floors. "Cool place. Lots of character."

"It was built in 1905 but has gone through many updates since then. The former owners of my condo kept the architectural details when they remodeled. When I saw it during an open house, I fell in love and made an offer on the spot." Paige wasn't ready to say goodbye, but she didn't feel like inviting him up, either. That might be too much. "Well, it's getting colder, and you need to get to your car. Thanks for hanging out with me tonight. It was a nice way to cap off the weekend."

"We can do it again next week."

"It's a date." Heat pooled in her cheeks. "Er, plan."

He laughed. "Either works."

If this were a date, a kiss would happen. Either by her or him. But it wasn't a date, so she wouldn't. Hugging him probably wasn't a good idea, either, even if it would be one of gratitude. She pulled out her key ring from her purse.

"I'll be in touch soon," he said.

"Okay." She stared at him as if transfixed. Funny, but he was looking at her the same way.

A horn honked on the street around the corner. The noise jolted her back to reality. She'd better get inside before she did or said something she might regret. Focusing on the door, she stuck her key in and opened it. "Goodnight, Wes."

* * *

I didn't say goodnight.

Heading toward the coffee shop, Wes groaned. He'd enjoyed being with Paige, but he felt off. Uncertain. Stupid. He'd spoken with some of the richest and most powerful people in the world. But none made him as nervous as she had.

Why?

An SUV double-parked on the street. As the passenger window rolled down, the sound of Christmas music grew louder. Craig, a member of Wes's security team, smiled. "A little cold for a stroll."

"Brisk air is good for the lungs," Wes replied.

"Until you wind up with pneumonia."

Craig was in his late forties with salt-and-pepper hair and a muscular frame. He'd followed them from the hospital to the coffee shop and then to her condo. Wes barely paid attention to the guys anymore. They were just part of his life, but Paige hadn't seemed to notice.

"Ready to go home?" Craig asked.

"Yes." Wes slid into the back seat and shut the door. Welcome heat surrounded him. "Didn't mean to keep you out so long."

"It's my job." Craig glanced in the rearview mirror. "You're smiling big. You must have had fun."

"I did."

Tonight hadn't turned out as Wes expected, but he enjoyed getting to know Paige. Saturday night would be more bearable with her at the dinner.

"She's pretty," Craig said in a matter-of-fact tone.

"We weren't on a date." If they had been, Wes would have kissed Paige. That would have been a nice way to end…

No, he shouldn't go there.

"Didn't say it was." Craig sounded like he was trying not to laugh, which was typical for the former Special Forces staff sergeant. "But she's still pretty."

Paige was. Fresh-faced rather than made up. "Don't let your wife hear that."

"I'm married, not dead." A new song played on the radio. Craig tapped his fingers against the steering wheel to the strains of "Sleigh Ride." "My wife and I have an agreement. We can each look all we want but no touching. That's served us well the past twenty-odd years."

"Good to know." Not that Wes needed an arrangement like that or would anytime soon. Throughout his twenties and early thirties, he'd dated casually. And then he'd met Annabelle.

Knots filled his stomach.

Wes pulled out his phone. He'd silenced it while he was playing Santa.

Text after text appeared on the screen.

His pulse kicked up. His hand shook.

Had something happened?

He unlocked the phone and scrolled to the first message.

Henry: *Wes might bring a plus-one to Saturday's dinner.*
Kieran: *Who is she?*
Mason: *It's about time.*
Adam: *Let Wes do things on his own time.*
Blaise: *Is it the woman Hadley introduced him to?*
Dash: *Maybe I can still win the bet?*
Brett: *Wes will tell us if he's bringing someone.*
Henry: *Is your goal in life, Brett Matthews, to take away all my fun?*
Brett: *You'll thank me when you're old and gray, Henry.*
Henry: *You mean when I'm a silver fox.*
Mason: *Tell us more about Wes's date.*

Wes groaned. Okay, he was relieved nothing bad had happened to anyone, but he hadn't expected their group chat to turn into a discussion about his social life or the lack of one.

Craig glanced over his shoulder. "You okay, Wes?"

"Yes, it's just…Henry."

He laughed. "Say no more."

Wes returned to the messages.

Dash: *I thought Wes was taking a break from dating.*

Blaise: *He was still on a break last week when Hadley spoke with him.*

Kieran: *Maybe he changed his mind.*

Henry: *Wes is trying to figure out what he wants.*

Mason: *I hope it's this woman. We need him to marry. Dash, too. That way, the bet's called off, and we split the fund.*

Dash: *Marriage isn't part of my five-year plan. It's only recently been added to my vocabulary thanks to you lovesick fools.*

Adam: *Does Raina know this?*

Dash: *I'm pretty sure I told her.*

Mason: *Which means we'll be getting a wedding invitation soon.*

Brett: *You should mention how you feel again, Dash. Raina seems really into you.*

Kieran: *Let's get back on topic. I want to know who Wes is asking out.*

Henry: *I know the lucky lady, and he should have asked her by now.*

Wes needed to stop them before they—well, Henry with an assist from Mason—had his life decided and non-existent children named. He tapped on his screen and sent a reply.

Wes: *She's not my date. I needed a plus-one.*
Henry: *I take it she said yes!!!!*
Mason: *Plus-ones can turn into more. A wife, even.*
Henry: *That's the first intelligent thing you've said in three days. Good job, Mase.*
Dash: *Tell us who she is.*

Wes gritted his teeth. He couldn't have one evening without everyone wanting to know everything. But then again, he was guilty of doing the same to the others.

Wes: *Paige Regis.*
Blaise: *Dr. Regis? Your oncologist?*
Henry: *Her specialty is hematology-oncology.*
Kieran: *Not an obvious choice for a plus-one, but good for you, Wes.*
Dash: *She's smart.*
Mason: *She's hot.*
Adam: *Mase!*
Mason: *She is. I'm just the only one brave enough to admit it.*

Brett: *Not sure I'd call it brave.*

Wes rolled his eyes. Maybe asking Paige to go on Saturday hadn't been such a good idea. His friends were as close as brothers, which meant they ribbed each other and argued like family.

Wes: *I'm almost home. Later.*
Dash: *We want to know more.*
Mason: *Dating again is a big deal.*
Adam: *Wes said not a date.*
Mason: *Semantics. I can see the two of them together.*
Henry: *You may be onto something, Mase.*
Kieran: *Stop encouraging him!*
Brett: *Don't encourage Henry, either.*
Henry: *I'm right here.*

Blowing out a breath, Wes closed the app. He would rather replay the evening with Paige than listen to his friends bicker about his upcoming non-date.

Although Wes should make plans for Saturday. He wanted to give Paige a taste of Hood Hamlet. First on his list was a call to Muffy, who owned the coffee shop, to ask if she served peppermint hot chocolate. If not, he'd pay her to add it to the menu for the day.

Craig turned on to Wes's street. They were almost home.

His phone rang. Based on the timing, he didn't have to look at the screen to know who it was. "What do you want, Henry?"

"She said yes!"

The guy had reverted to a teenager. Ridiculous, but Wes answered because Henry was a friend despite how annoying he could be at times. "Paige did."

Henry whistled. "You're on a first-name basis now. Excellent."

Ugh. Wes shook his head. Maybe *teenager* was too generous for Henry. "How old are you again?"

"Younger than you," Henry joked. In the background, ice cubes clinked against glass. "So what else happened after I left?"

"We spoke." Wes wasn't sure how much he wanted to say. "She's excited to meet potential donors, so thanks for that idea."

"And?" Henry's nosiness was showing.

Wes would not play. "Nothing."

"Don't nothing me." The three words came out sharp. "I left hours ago. You're just getting home. Where have you been?"

If Henry put as much effort into something more productive than being nosey, he could change the world. "I went to a coffee shop."

"With Paige."

It wasn't a question, so Wes didn't feel obligated to answer. His garage door opened.

"Wes?" Henry asked.

"I'm here." Wes tried to sound nonchalant.

"Have you been with Paige this entire time?"

Henry's surprised tone grated.

Part of Wes wanted to answer, but he didn't want to deal with the consequences of doing that. "Maybe."

"I could ask Wonderkid to check his GPS beta tracker prototype to see where you've been tonight."

Wes growled. "Dash's tracker isn't for your amusement or to appease your curiosity."

"Then answer my question." No doubt a smug smile was on Henry's face.

"Paige and I went to a coffee shop." That was all Wes was going to admit to.

"Did you kiss her?" Henry asked in a singsong voice.

Wes stared at the phone in disbelief. "Seriously?"

"It's Christmastime, Mr. Scrooge," Henry countered. "Mistletoe is everywhere."

"No mistletoe tonight." The words shot out. Mistletoe and Paige didn't belong in the same sentence.

"Saturday, then."

"Not. A. Date." Wes ground out the words. "If you're trying to play matchmaker, I'll tell Brett."

Henry gasped. "You wouldn't dare."

"Try me," Wes challenged. "Brett and Laurel said no fixing anyone up until your birthday. That's in April, not December. Do they know you introduced Blaise and Hadley?"

"An introduction is not matchmaking." If Henry was trying to appear innocent, he was failing.

Wes laughed. "To everyone else on this planet, no, but you are in a league of your own."

"Thank you."

"It wasn't a compliment," Wes mumbled.

"I heard that."

"Good, because you need to back off where Paige is concerned," Wes lectured. "I don't want you to embarrass her on Saturday night."

"I wouldn't," Henry said a little too quickly.

The car came to a stop in the garage. Wes unbuckled his seat belt. "You would and not even realize what you said."

A beat passed. And another. "I'll be especially careful where she's concerned."

"Thank you."

"You're welcome."

Silence filled the line.

That meant Henry was thinking or plotting. Maybe a combination of the two. "What?"

"You've had a break from dating. It's okay if you like Dr. Regis and want to go out with her," Henry said, his voice softer than before. "The only one holding you back is Annabelle. Not every woman is like her. The right one is out there, waiting for you."

A lump burned in Wes's throat. He tried to swallow around it. Tried and failed.

"Thanks," he croaked.

"Think about it," Henry urged.

Wes made a non-committal grunt, said bye, and

disconnected from the call. He went into the house. The lights were on, but it was so quiet.

Too quiet.

He went upstairs, each step reminding him of the last time Annabelle had been here.

The tears.

Hers.

And his.

Wes went into his bedroom. A heaviness overtook him. His stomach churned, making him relieved he ate little at the party.

Thoughts of Annabelle swirled.

She wasn't as bad as everyone thought, but his friends hated her.

The only problem?

Annabelle hadn't left him because of his cancer. She'd wanted to stay with him—marry him—but Wes hadn't believed her. Hadn't thought she could handle his cancer. Hadn't trusted she loved him enough.

The cancer had been the catalyst for their breakup, but there had been bigger issues than that. He'd wanted her to prove her love and show him she wasn't after his money, but his accusations and suspicions had driven them apart.

He'd pushed her away, giving her no reason to stay with him.

Wes had never meant for Annabelle to become the villain in their breakup, but he'd been at such a low point, emotionally and physically, he allowed her to take the blame, never correcting others.

Never telling them the entire story.

Never apologizing before she moved away to start over where so many people didn't hate her.

Why wasn't he dating?

Wes didn't deserve to be in a happy relationship. Like the companies he purchased and decimated without a second thought, he'd done the same thing to his girlfriend who'd loved him. He'd broken her heart and driven her out of the town she'd called home.

Yes, he was working to be a better person, but he didn't trust himself to get involved again. He didn't want to hurt another woman the way he'd hurt Annabelle. Which might explain why he'd felt so off tonight. Something about Paige made him want to forget his resolve, but he couldn't.

Dr. Paige Regis deserved better. She was in a class by herself. No matter what Wes did—hours playing Santa or donating millions—he would never be worthy of someone like her.

Chapter Five

On Wednesday, Paige finished her appointments fifty minutes behind schedule. Not bad considering two patients had to be fit in. Replying to emails was the only thing she had left to do before heading to the hospital. Unfortunately, the task was taking her longer than usual. The reason—Wes Lockhart.

He hadn't been in touch, but that didn't concern her. Not much anyway. Even working fewer hours than before, he had to be busy. Besides, his foundation had contacted the hospital about paying his pledge.

Paige was both delighted and relieved by the donation. No more fundraising. She only wished Wes wouldn't keep popping into her mind so much. That was distracting and strange. She didn't like it.

Must be gratitude over the twenty-five million.

That was the only reason that made sense.

A knock sounded on her door before her nurse, Lydia, stuck her head into the office. "Mr. Chaffey is settled in his room."

A patient had taken a turn for the worst. Nothing new, unfortunately, but unexpected after Dexter Chaffey's last scan and tests. "I'll be heading over there shortly."

"No one came with him."

The "again" was left unspoken but implied. An absurd situation given his family lived locally, but they appeared more concerned with their own lives than that of their father, brother, uncle, and grandfather, who had lost his wife two years ago to a heart attack.

So sad.

"Did someone contact the volunteer office?" Paige asked.

"Yes, and Mr. Chaffey is now on the list."

At least Dexter would have a visitor during his stay. "Thank you."

Lydia shook her head. "If he was my grandpa—"

"But he's not." Paige used her firm doctor's tone, the one she reverted to when patients didn't want to follow her directions.

The nurse frowned. "I know, but I'd like to have a word with his kids and grandkids."

"Same." Paige tried not to let a patient's personal

situation affect her. This one, however, frustrated her. "But you can't force people to care. Not even about their own family."

"They'll regret ignoring him someday."

"They will, but that's on them." Dexter had tried so hard not to be a burden to his family after his wife's death that they'd forgotten him in his time of need. None of his children accompanied him to appointments or visited him when he was in the hospital. He used a ride service for his chemo treatments. Thinking about how alone he must feel hurt her heart. "I just wish Dexter didn't have to pay the price, too."

Lydia nodded. "Have a good evening."

A few minutes later, Paige sent her final reply. Now, she could go to the cancer care unit. As she reached for her coat, her cell phone buzzed with a text notification.

Glancing at the screen, she smiled.

Wes: *The foundation will be making the donation.*
Paige: *Thank you.*
Wes: *About Saturday, I had an idea.*
Paige: *Is that a good thing or a bad thing?*
Wes: *Looks as if medical school left your humerus bone intact.*
Paige: *Har-har-har.*
Paige: *So what's your idea?*
Wes: *Are you off all weekend?*
Paige: *Yes.*

Wes: *People are staying overnight after the dinner. You should, too.*

Paige's heart lodged in her throat. What did staying overnight entail? A hundred thoughts ran through her mind. Questions swirled.

She reread his text. Took a calming breath. Relaxed.

This wasn't an invitation to a sleepover. More of a suggestion to stay in Hood Hamlet. A vague one.

Paige typed a reply.

Paige: *Could we talk about this?*
Wes: *Calling now.*

She answered on the first ring. "Hey."

"I should have just called, but it's been a crazy day so I went with a text." He sounded tired. More worn out than the bone-weariness crippling fatigue that had plagued him when he'd had cancer. "Is this a good time for you?"

"Yes."

"So my idea…" He took a breath. "If you drive up early on Saturday morning, we can spend the day at the Christmas Magic celebration. Everyone is staying overnight in Hood Hamlet after the dinner. They'll want to have brunch on Sunday, so if you stay, too, that will give you another chance to get to know people better."

Paige released the breath she hadn't realized she was holding.

This was a business invitation—a way to help her and the cancer center. Except, her chest tightened as if a fifty-pound weight bore down on her.

Ridiculous.

She shouldn't be disappointed that this wasn't...a personal invite. She needed to jump on the opportunity for the cancer center.

"Sounds great." She kept her tone light. "Where should I book a room?"

"You can stay with me. Half are staying with me. The others will be at Henry's. Our places are on the same street."

Paige assumed Wes's house was big, but... "I don't want to impose."

"You aren't," he said without missing a beat. "You'll never find a room in town this close to the event."

He was probably right.

So why was she hesitating?

She wanted to get to know his friends. He was offering her a place to stay. There appeared to be no quid pro quo involved.

"Okay," she said finally. "I'd rather not make the long drive back late at night."

"I'll text you my address up there."

"Thanks." She remembered reading a short article about the Christmas Magic celebration. "Do I need to bring anything since the dinner is a benefit?"

"A ticket and an unwrapped toy donation are required, but I'm going shopping tomorrow for ours."

Ours.

Goose bumps prickled her skin. She clutched her phone tighter. "If you want help, let me know."

The words burst out.

"Do you know what toys kids like?" Wes asked.

"I've shopped for my brother's kids." She'd ordered gifts for them and her family on Sunday morning. She'd even bought herself something.

"Then, I'd appreciate the help," he said happily. "Can you go shopping with me tomorrow night?"

"Yes." After all Wes was doing for her, Paige wanted to help him. She'd researched enough of this year's hot toys to know the good ones and the must-haves. "But I'm not sure what time I'll finish working."

"That's fine. Stores are open later since it's December."

He appeared to be flexible about the time. "I can text you when I get off."

"Sounds good."

It did. "Have a great rest of the day."

"You, too. See you tomorrow." He disconnected from the call.

Paige shoved her phone into her jacket pocket. Toy shopping wasn't a date, but anticipation shot to her toes.

* * *

As Wes entered the mall the next night, his muscles twitched. Not a case of nerves, more a touch of…uncertainty. He'd gotten out of the habit of going to malls and big stores. Too many people with germs. Even now when that didn't matter, he worried—so he found smaller shops, boutiques, and ordering online were more comfortable. When he needed clothing alterations, his tailor came to him.

Who was he kidding? Everyone came to Wes if he asked.

And paid.

He continued walking farther into the mall. It might be a weeknight, but that hadn't kept holiday shoppers away. They juggled bags while weaving their way through the crowd-packed place.

People spoke over the Christmas music playing. These weren't traditional carols, but modern tunes with a faster beat and stronger baseline. Shiny decorations sparkled and glowed from the ceiling and on the floor. Lighted garlands hung from the upper floor's railing.

A woman wearing a Santa hat smiled at him. "Merry Christmas."

Wes opened his mouth to repeat the words, but nothing came out. He nodded instead.

Three teenagers with red glowing noses and holding pink shopping bags walked past. A mom chased a toddler in an elf suit. Somewhere carolers sang, a different song from the music playing from the mall's speakers.

The people, the sights, and the sounds overwhelmed him.

His stomach knotted. Why hadn't he ordered the toys online and chosen same-day pickup?

"Go ahead and say it," Craig said, walking a half-step behind him. "You're thinking it."

Yeah, Wes was. He didn't care who heard him. "Bah humbug."

Craig snickered. "Knew it."

"I prefer an old-fashioned Christmas, not…" Wes glanced around and grimaced. "Over-the-top glitz and commercialism."

"Something like Hood Hamlet."

"Exactly like Hood Hamlet." Wes couldn't wait to be there on Friday night. His staff would have the lodge clean and ready, but he wanted to have a few special surprises in place to make Paige's time there memorable.

A large lighted Christmas tree caught his eye. This wasn't as tall as the one in the center of the mall. Paper ornaments with writing on them hung from the branches. He read one—Age 8: A child's tablet.

Wes froze.

"You okay?" Craig asked.

"This is a giving tree?"

"Yes."

Wes hadn't seen one in years. He scanned other tags—Age 3: Wooden train, Age 10: Chess set, Age 5: Baby doll. Each tag listed an age and a toy.

Toys for kids in need.

Blaise Mortenson, his closest friend, came to mind.

What had Christmas been like for Blaise with addicts for parents? Had he received gifts under the tree from Santa? Had a charity stepped in? Or had his family even celebrated the holiday?

Wes's chest tightened.

The urge to grab every tag was strong, something he wanted to do for a younger Blaise and for himself. Wes reached forward.

"It's the second week of December," Craig said. "There's plenty of time left for people to take tags."

Wes lowered his arm to his side, but his gaze remained locked on the tags. A nine-year-old wanted a jigsaw puzzle. Was that the only gift they wanted? Would that be all they received under their tree? Did they even have a tree?

The questions swirled in his brain. "I could…"

"You could, but you also have the foundation."

The foundation. That gave him an idea. "I'll talk to Sadie."

Except then he wouldn't be personally involved as Henry recommended.

Craig started to speak but stopped himself.

"What?" Wes asked.

Craig kept his lips pressed together.

Wes shook his head. "You might as well tell me because I'll get it out of you, eventually."

Craig squared his shoulders. "You don't have to save the world."

"I know." But Wes wanted—needed—to do…something. He had to make the most of being in remission. He couldn't right all the wrongs he'd done or the people he'd hurt, but he could help others. Which was why he removed three tags from the tree. "I'm taking these. I'll be in the toy store, anyway."

"You should be there already." Craig sounded more amused than annoyed. "Dr. Regis is waiting for you."

Paige was here? Wes's heart kicked up a notch. "Where?"

"Your date is up ahead."

Wes huffed. "Not a date."

Craig coughed. "My bad."

Yeah, right.

Paige faced the toy shop's window display. She wore a green sweater under a quilted parka vest and black leggings tucked into suede boots. A single braid hung past her shoulders.

"Paige," Wes called.

As she turned toward him, a smile spread across her face. "Hi."

Wes's breath caught in his throat.

Beautiful.

Not a date, he reminded himself. "You beat me here."

Her mouth slanted. "I didn't realize it was a competition."

"It's not."

Though he and his friends could turn anything into one. That was how they ended up with the last-single-man-standing bet. Each put ten million dollars into a fund Blaise used to beta test his latest algorithm. The amount surpassed the five-hundred-million mark. Winner would take all, but the money was only the icing. Bragging rights held more value to Wes.

"I forget that sometimes," he added.

"You and your friends like to compete."

It wasn't a question. "We do, but how do you know that?"

Her gaze glimmered with mischief. "I remember a race to see who could finish a sudoku puzzle the fastest during one of your treatments. Things became a bit…heated."

Wes laughed. That would have been Blaise, who always needed to win. Though the guy had chosen love—and Hadley—over winning the bet. "It wasn't too heated because security wasn't called."

"I believe that threat was made at least once," she teased.

Heat flooded Wes's face. "Your memory is correct, but in my defense, it made the chemo go quicker."

"Whatever it takes." She sounded sincere.

His health, then or now, wasn't something he wanted to discuss. "So toys…"

"Many of the top ten toys are sold out," she said in that doctor tone of hers he'd relied upon as much as oxygen when things had been difficult. "Board games are popular. You can never go wrong with a LEGO set."

"I loved those when I was a kid. Do you think…?"

"It's a great toy, and not only for children. I knew someone in his forties who loved them, too."

Her nostalgic tone made Wes wonder who. And she'd spoken in past tense. Possibly a patient or family member.

"We need two toys for the dinner. And…" He held up the three gift requests. "These from the mall's giving tree."

Tilting her head, she studied him as if he were a lab rat. "That's sweet of you to do."

"It's nothing." He could do so much more.

"No, it's something," she countered. "You keep surprising me, Wes Lockhart."

Her compliment made him straighten, but he hoped she liked him doing that. "Thanks."

She took the three tags and read them. "We can go down each aisle and see if anything looks interesting to you."

"Okay." He glanced at Craig. "Paige, this is Craig, my driver. He'll help us carry things."

Paige extended her arm to shake Craig's hand. "Nice to meet you."

Craig flashed a charming smile. "The pleasure is all mine."

The bodyguard's flirty tone grated on Wes.

"Ready to shop?" he asked.

She nodded.

Wes followed her inside. They went to the first aisle, which contained baby items and stuffed animals.

The next aisle was a kaleidoscope of pinks and purples—dolls, accessories, and dress-up clothing. The campers and townhomes were interesting, but the dolls weren't babies.

Paige tapped his shoulder. "One of these would be good."

The first box contained an individual doll with a blanket, bottle, and outfit. Two others were sets that had more accessories. He had no idea what would be best. "Which one?"

She reread one of the paper ornaments. "The child is five, so I suggest a set. More to play with, but the largest box has small items which might get lost."

He studied each before pulling a medium-sized set from the shelf. "This one doesn't have as many accessories, but it has more clothing and a baby carrier."

She nodded. "Good choice."

His mouth slanted. "Is this a test?"

"No." She laughed. "Your money. Your choice. I'm just here to offer suggestions."

He handed the box to Craig. "Tell me which you'd purchase."

She smiled. "You're one for one."

Craig's smile widened, but he remained quiet. Wes hoped the bodyguard stayed that way.

The next row was full of games. He searched shelves. "I'm not seeing a chess set."

"This is where it would be." She went up on her tiptoes and then bent over to the lowest shelf. "Down here."

"No wonder it was hard to find." As Wes reached for the one that caught his eye, his hand brushed Paige's. Heat ignited at the point of contact.

She jerked hers away as if burned.

What had Craig said about looking not touching? Wes needed to remember that.

He pulled out the two sets. One was for beginners. Perfectly fine, but he preferred the one in a wooden case with a nicer board and pieces.

"This one." He handed the box to Craig.

Little kid toys were in the next aisle, including a wooden train set. Wes eyed them with confusion. "They are all cool. How do you pick just one?"

"The child is three. Any set will be fine."

Except Wes wanted to purchase the perfect one. "Which would you choose?"

"I've never had a train, but my nephew was a huge Thomas the Tank Engine fan when he was that age." She pointed to a larger set. "That's the closest to what he had. It was a well-loved and played-with toy."

"How many nieces and nephews do you have?"

"Three." Affection shone in her eyes. "Two nephews and one niece. They are the cutest. They live on the East Coast, so I don't see them often, but when I do, I love to spoil them rotten."

"Lucky kids."

"Lucky aunt."

His gaze held hers. The connection flowing between them made him want to move closer. Touch her.

No touching. Only looking.

He removed a set from the shelf.

"Craig only has two hands so I'll carry this." Wes held the box like a shield as if it could keep him from doing something stupid where Dr. Paige Regis was concerned. "What's next?"

Amusement glimmered in her eyes. "Picking out the two gifts for the dinner."

Those presents were the reason they were here. "Let's see what's on the next row."

As soon as he turned the corner, he froze. Building blocks, bricks, sticks, and logs of every kind filled the shelves. Individual pieces and a variety of themed sets. "Now we're talking."

"Do any catch your eye?" she asked.

"All of them," he joked.

"I don't think you're kidding," she teased. "Must be the engineer in you."

His gaze jerked to hers. "You know what my degree is?"

Paige nodded. "You and your company are well-known around town. I pay attention to the local news."

He stood taller until he realized she might have heard the rumors about his business dealings and private life, too. He forced his shoulders not to droop. "Not everything reported is true."

"They didn't lie about your degrees, right?"

His muscles bunched into tight balls. She used the plural, which meant she likely knew about his MBA. What else had she heard? "No, but the other stuff…"

Paige touched his arm, a gesture of comfort but one he relished. "You're a good man, Wes. I know better than to listen to gossip or innuendo."

Emotion clogged his throat. He didn't want Paige to think badly of him. Though if she had or did, she'd never let it show.

Because she's a doctor and a professional.

Was that all she was being now?

He didn't want to know the answer.

Wes swallowed. "Thanks."

She smiled softly before lowering her hand. "You're welcome."

He removed a large box from the shelf. It was a

set from a hit movie franchise that had a premiere coming up later this month. "What do you think of this one?"

She grinned. "Perfect. Do you want to donate two or find something else for the second toy?"

Two would make this easy, and they could get out of there. But then what? Say goodbye to Paige until Saturday. Wes wasn't ready to do that.

"One is good." He would have Eliza order more sets online and have them delivered to the Hood Hamlet Fire Station as an anonymous donation. "Let's see what else is here."

A mix of science kits and electronic items filled the shelves.

As Paige surveyed the toys, her face lit up. "When I was a kid, I received a circuit board set. It was my absolute favorite."

"Not a microscope kit?"

She shook her head. "I didn't think about becoming a doctor until I was in high school."

"What made you want to study medicine?"

"My best friend's mom was diagnosed with leukemia. I helped as much as I could. Visited her in the hospital."

"Did she…?"

"She died two years after her diagnosis."

When he'd gone into remission, but not Zeke. "I'm sorry."

"Thanks, but going through that set me on a path

that brought me here." She didn't sound upset or filled with regret. "My friend lives in Southern California now. She's supported me every step of the way and says her mom would be proud."

Wes was proud of Paige. A tragedy had led her to saving lives, including his. A lump formed in his throat. "I'm sure."

Paige focused on the kits. "Any of these would be great."

She wanted to change the subject. That was fine with Wes, but he was glad he'd learned something else about her. He checked the different products and then…

One featuring a blue robot grabbed his attention. Excitement shot through him. "I read about this toy. It's won awards."

"A robot! That would be cool."

"It would." As he read the features listed on the box, longing built inside him. He would have loved a toy like this when he was younger. But then again, his family called him a nerd.

"The way you're eyeing the robot makes me wonder if you want one, too." She sounded amused.

Busted. He laughed. "One will be enough, but I might have to ask Santa for my own."

A toy that taught basic coding skills and was fun belonged on his list. All his friends' lists, too.

Geeks r us.

She took a box from the shelf. "Do you need

anything else?"

"I'm finished buying my family gifts."

"Me, too. I did everything online."

"I did something similar." He'd discovered Cassandra's Attic, an independent bookstore in San Francisco, through Brett Matthews. The shop's book concierge had helped him pick out a special gift for each person on his list. "Everyone is getting a book this year."

Paige clutched the robot's box. "Books are the best presents."

"I hope my friends and family enjoy theirs."

"It's a gift," she said. "How could they not enjoy it?"

"I agree." His family, however, could be hard on a present-giver, but if they weren't happy with a special- or limited-edition book, that was their problem, not his.

After he paid, they exited the store. "Thanks for coming with me tonight. Toy buying was easier than I thought it would be."

"All I did was walk with you and share my opinion. You did the rest."

"It was a team effort." He glanced at the time. "Want to grab dinner?"

A range of emotions flashed in her eyes. He had a hard time keeping up with each, but he hadn't missed the longing. That told him she enjoyed spending time with him as much as he did with her.

Paige opened her mouth but then closed it. She tried again. "Thanks, but I need to go home."

What? His breath hitched. He was sure she would go to dinner. But he couldn't force her to stay.

"I have some work to do," she replied as if an excuse would make her rejection any better.

"Okay." Except it wasn't. Wes wanted to have dinner with her. "Thanks for your help."

She appeared as if she wanted to say something but blew out a breath instead. "You're welcome."

"I'll take your bag," Craig said to her.

Paige handed it over. "See you on Saturday."

Wes nodded, but he didn't want to wait to see her on Saturday. Maybe he could change that…

Nope. That was what old Wes would do. Flash his money. Crank up the charm. Convince someone to do what he wanted.

"I hope you get everything done quickly." The words tasted like sand, but they were the correct ones to say.

"Bye," she said.

As he watched Paige walk away, his insides deflated.

Craig nudged him. "Let's get these toys home."

Wes could eat dinner there, but eating by himself was getting old. Which was why he'd invited Paige out. He was tired of being alone. If only he could fix that.

But how, when he didn't want to date anyone?

Chapter Six

After leaving Portland, Paige's drive to Hood Hamlet was relatively free of traffic. A pleasant surprise on a Saturday. She hadn't known how many people would head to Mount Hood this morning, which was why she'd left early.

As she drove east, gaining elevation with each mile, the piles of snow lining the side of Highway 26 became higher, but the road remained clear. That, however, didn't lessen the knot in her stomach—one that had been there since Thursday night.

Thanks, but I need to go home.

Even though Paige had wanted to go to dinner with Wes, the words had shot out of her mouth before she could stop them.

The reason—fear.

She'd been afraid of spending more time with him.

Paige gripped the steering wheel. Being with Wes at the toy store had been fun. More fun than she'd had in weeks. The way he wanted to pick the right gift endeared him to her. That, however, worried her because a glance or a smile left her unsettled. Which meant…

I have a crush on Wes.

Paige half laughed. Shook her head. Turned up the radio to hear "Home for the Holidays" better.

Having a crush at her age was ridiculous. But add in who the object of her affections was…

She blew out a breath as if she could expel the crush as easily.

No reason to worry, though. She had a reason for feeling this way.

Wes Lockhart was gorgeous, kind, and rich. By donating money to the cancer center, he was making her Christmas wish come true.

Who wouldn't crush on him?

But she'd need to keep her attraction hidden. No staring at him no matter how handsome he looked. No sighing. Forget swooning. Otherwise, she would make a fool out of herself.

A large sign on the side of the highway read *Hood Hamlet.* Her directions were to Wes's house, but she would see the town soon enough when they attended the Christmas Magic celebration.

She followed the directions on the map app, leaving the highway. Tall pine trees with snow-laden branches lined the sides of the street. Add in the clear blue sky overhead and she felt as if she'd entered a winter wonderland.

"Turn left on to Hamlet Heights Lane," the voice on her phone instructed.

Paige did.

A log cabin sat on the right. Though "cabin" didn't describe the immense size. This was more like a mountain lodge, something she would see on HGTV or in a home magazine.

She drove past other lodges until she reached the end of the road. Snow covered the yard, but the driveway was clear. She pulled into it.

Wes's house was larger than the other seven. White lights dangled from the eaves, outlining the roofline. A holly garland wrapped around a wooden lamppost. A large wreath with a red bow hung on the front door.

Gorgeous.

Like something out of a Christmas movie.

Paige turned off the engine, pulled the key from the ignition, and slid from the car. The cold temperature brought a shiver. The snow in the yard glistened. The sharp scent of pine lingered on the crisp air.

She grabbed her purse and bag from the back seat. As she went to the front door, she saw pinecones and holly in the large wreath. Paige rang the doorbell.

Bells chimed.

"Fancy."

The door opened. Wes wore jeans, a sweater, and wool socks. No shoes. Nothing out of the ordinary, but on him, the outfit looked like high fashion. Yes, she'd always considered Wes attractive, but he'd been her patient so seeing him as anything else would have been wrong. But now…

He grinned. "You made it."

Her pulse sped up. She nodded.

Wes opened the door wider. "Come in."

As soon as she crossed the threshold into the two-story foyer, warmth enveloped her. The scent of fresh-baked cookies filled the air.

Wood floors and earth tone décor gave the home a welcoming feel. To her right was an office behind glass doors, but then the entryway opened up to an expansive living area with a great room, dining area, and gourmet kitchen. A lighted garland covered the wood banister leading to the second floor.

This was like a movie. Wes was the star, but she was no lead actress. More like the loyal friend and confidant.

Paige swallowed a laugh. "Your house is amazing."

"Thanks." He closed the door. "Let me take your coat before you overheat. The caretaker keeps the lodge warm."

"Toasty and cozy." She set her bag and purse on the floor before shrugging off her puffy jacket. "Well, for a big house."

Wes hung up her coat on a hook. "Dash calls this place a log cabin on steroids."

A valid description. Paige recognized the name. She'd meant to research his friends but had worked late last night. Truth was, she remembered names better than faces, but she would take a shot. "Is Dash the younger guy? Tall and thin who brought video games for you to play?"

Wes smiled as if he was remembering. "That's him. He'll be at the dinner tonight with his girlfriend. How was the drive?"

"Great." She followed him into the massive living area that ran the width of the house. "No traffic."

"You beat the rush." He motioned to the combination kitchen/dining/living space. "The theater is upstairs, but I spend most of my time in here. The fridge is stocked, so is the bar. Please make yourself at home."

A huge island separated the gourmet kitchen from the dining area. The wood cabinets and butcher block countertops softened the more contemporary stainless steel appliances. Two decorations sat on the breakfast bar. A moose holding a chalkboard that read "*Let it snow!*" was on one side of the counter. A coordinating cookie jar had been placed on the other corner.

"This is a chef's dream kitchen." She wanted to peek inside each cabinet. "Do you enjoy cooking?"

Mischief gleamed in his eyes. "Let's just say I can cook, but I prefer to leave it to others."

He had the means to do that. But so did she to a lesser extent. "I have a freezer full of healthy meals I ordered so I only have to heat them up if I've had a busy day."

A pretty poinsettia centerpiece sat in the middle of the large dining table that seated sixteen. The style was more casual than formal but screamed quality. Interestingly, the lodge felt more like a family home than a party palace, given Wes's single status and reputation.

"That's a big table," she said.

"I wanted to have room for everyone."

Something clicked in her brain. "Aren't there just six of you?"

"Six of us known as the billionaires of Silicon Forest, but there's also Henry Davenport and Brett Matthews who are close friends."

She did a quick calculation in her head. "Sixteen spots for when everyone is paired up."

Wes's cheeks turned an adorable shade of pink. "It seemed like a good idea."

"It is." Wes had his parents and his friends. Two separate support groups. Two families. One by blood. The other by choice. If only everyone could be so fortunate.

She ran her fingertips over the smooth wood. "You want your family at the same table."

He opened his mouth, but no words came out. He nodded.

Paige went into the great room, past the leather couch with a colorful red and green throw tossed over the arm, to the stone fireplace. No logs burned, but she imagined wood crackling and flames dancing. "I love the fireplace."

"I designed it myself," he said, proudly.

"You're a man of hidden talents."

"I know what I like. What I want." He raised his chin. "I make it happen."

His drive—determination—appealed to her. "You nailed this."

On top of the wood mantel, silver and gold ornaments and tall red candles sat on top of pine branches. A single stocking with the letter W embroidered in red on the white cuff hung below.

Seeing only one stocking surprised her. "Do you spend Christmas here?"

"Christmas Eve." He straightened a throw pillow on an oversized chair. "Hood Hamlet is where you can experience a quintessential small-town Christmas. The church puts on a Nativity pageant with kids playing the various parts, and the brewpub hosts a Christmas Eve buffet. I eat there so my staff can have the night off. I invite whoever will be on their own to join me."

Paige was tempted to raise her hand, but she was on call and didn't want to be this far away from the hospital. Not that she expected an invitation. But being asked might be nice, even if she would say no.

"We have a big breakfast on Christmas morning. That afternoon, I'll drive back to Portland for my family's Christmas dinner," he added. "At least that's what I used to do. The last two years have been different."

Because of the cancer. "You'll get your traditions back, and maybe make a new one or two."

"I'm planning on it." His gaze met hers. "Starting today."

Her heart bumped.

Paige didn't want to look away, but self-preservation made her turn her head. White lights twinkled on the tree, a thick red ribbon acted as garland, and multicolored shiny balls hung from the branches. A large gold star sat at the top, shimmering from the natural lighting coming in through the floor-to-ceiling windows. The decorations were simple, but the effect was charming.

"Your tree is beautiful." The sharp pine scent told her the Christmas tree was real, not artificial like the small one she still hadn't set up. "Did you cut it yourself?"

"No." He half laughed as if sharing an inside joke with himself. "The house was decorated when I arrived last night."

"If I lived here, I might keep a tree up all year and decorate it for each month or season." She touched a branch. No needles came off. "The bowed window was made for a Christmas tree."

"It was," he admitted. "I asked the architect to include an area to showcase a Christmas tree."

She would have never thought of doing something like that. "You *do* know what you want."

He nodded. "I'm comfortable at my place in Portland, but the lodge is home. We came here when I was younger. I always felt Hood Hamlet was where I'm meant to be. Except work has me in Portland."

"You might live here permanently someday."

"I hope so." A wistful expression formed on his face. "I shouldn't complain. Weekend getaways are better than nothing."

Ideas on how he could spend more time in Hood Hamlet ran through her head, but it wasn't her place to tell him what to do.

Wes headed into the kitchen and picked up a platter from the counter. "I forgot to offer you a cookie."

Gingerbread cookies, some decorated and others plain, filled the platter.

"Help yourself," he offered.

Paige was tempted except… "It's still morning."

"Cookies have similar ingredients to pancakes or waffles," he explained in a matter-of-fact tone. "Eggs, flour, butter. Some have milk."

"You could say the same about cake."

"I do during other times of the year, but cookies are one of the five food groups of Christmas along with fudge, eggnog, candy canes, and fruitcake. So you need to have one."

"Okay, I'm convinced."

"That was easier than I thought it would be."

"You're persuasive about cookies." She picked up a gingerbread man and bit off an arm. "Delicious."

He bowed. "Thank you."

"Wait." She glanced from the cookie to him. "I thought you let others cook."

"I do, but baking was a team effort." Wes sounded proud.

Paige didn't blame him. She took another bite but couldn't help but wonder who else was part of the team. He'd said he wasn't dating anyone and needed a plus-one for the benefit dinner. Unless he had met someone since then. The thought bothered her, way more than it should.

"Who else made the cookies?" she asked.

"Nora. She keeps the lodge clean and me fed. She's married to Jim, who is the caretaker." Affection filled Wes's voice. "We have a Christmas tradition of baking cookies whenever I'm up here in December."

"That's a tasty tradition." Paige ate the rest of the cookie.

"It is."

"So, is attending the festival another one of your traditions?" she asked.

"This is its third year, but a new experience for me. I've never been."

She realized why. He'd been sick the past two years in December. "You must make the most of it."

"I'm planning to." He glanced at his watch. "Our ride to town should be here shortly. Do you want to put your bag in your room? Hang up your clothes?"

She remembered her dress for tonight. "Please."

"There's a guest room above the garage with a separate entrance, but I'm giving that to Blaise and Hadley, who got married last month."

She followed him up the wide staircase. "Newlyweds."

He nodded. "One of four couples who married in the past five months. Three are staying here."

"That's…"

"A lot." He laughed. "Adam was first. Next was Kieran. Then Mason. And finally Blaise. The last three caught the garter at the previous wedding so if that string continues, Dash will be next."

"You mentioned he has a girlfriend."

"Raina," Wes replied. "She's great. Perfect for him. But they've only been dating a couple of months. Time will tell."

So that was what Wes had meant about him and Henry being the only single ones remaining.

"You're in the guest room next to me." Wes

pushed open a door that had been ajar. "If you need anything, please let me know."

Paige stepped inside to find not a bedroom but a mini-suite, complete with a sitting area and a bathroom. She'd grown up comfortable. Her parents had well-paying jobs so money had never been an issue, but this house was on another level. Wes and his friends lived in a different world. She didn't want to be intimidated, but she was.

"Hangers are in the closet," he added.

"Thanks."

"Come downstairs after you're finished." With that, he left the room.

Paige hung her dress and carried her toiletry bag into the bathroom. She didn't know whether or not to expect gold-plated fixtures, though those wouldn't fit the decorating scheme. She was happy to see a more rustic décor in soothing brown tones with wood-paneled walls, tile floor, and his and her vessel sinks on a wood countertop.

Back in the bedroom, she removed her gloves, hat, and scarf from her suitcase's side pocket, swung her purse strap over her shoulder, and went downstairs.

Wes tilted his head as if listening to something. "I hear our ride."

Paige hadn't heard a car. She pulled on her hat and gloves. "I'm ready."

They went outside. Hers was the only car parked

on the driveway. "Our ride…"

"Is waiting for us on the street." He led her down the driveway. She couldn't see the road because of the bushes and trees.

A bell jingled.

That was odd. "What…?"

"You'll see in a minute."

When she reached the end of the driveway, she froze. "It's a…"

"Sleigh."

A black horse wearing a harness covered with bells stood in front of the red and green sleigh decorated with garland. A driver in an old-fashioned stove-top hat, a cape, and a long scarf smiled at them.

"Is this our ride?" she asked.

He nodded. "Have you done this before?"

"No." She wiggled her toes because that was about to change. "Is a horse-drawn sleigh ride part of the Christmas Magic celebration?"

"It's part of yours."

Her pulse skittered. "Thank you."

Paige's voice sounded husky. She cleared her throat.

He held her hand. No skin touched because of their gloves, but warmth flowed up her arm.

"Hop in," he said.

She did and then sat on the padded bench.

Wes climbed up and sat next to her, his side against hers. "Not a lot of room."

"It's fine." Who was she kidding? This was perfect. "The day's only beginning, but I feel as if I'm starring in my own holiday movie."

Complete with a gorgeous hottie who was a billionaire.

He covered them with a thick blanket. "Warm enough?"

"Now I am."

The sleigh glided along the street. The horse's bells jingled, offering the perfect soundtrack. The only thing missing was snow falling from the sky, but the clear weather was better for the town's celebration.

She glanced at Wes's profile. So handsome and strong. "Do you do this often?"

"Sleigh rides?"

"Make people's wishes come true," she clarified.

His cheeks reddened. Or maybe that was from the cold.

"It's something new," he admitted. "But I'm enjoying myself."

"Well, let me say, you have mad skills." She stared at the winter landscape, but only felt warmth flowing through her veins. "We haven't arrived at the celebration, and today's already enchanted."

Was it wrong she felt that way about him, too?

He tapped the tip of her nose. "I hope you feel that way once you see the town."

As Paige enjoyed the scenery—and Wes—she lost

track of time. "This reminds me of Narnia in the wintertime."

"You've been there?" he joked.

"Many times, thanks to the books and movies."

The sleigh rounded a corner, and she fell into Wes. He held on to her.

Heat rushed up her neck. "Sorry about that."

"Not your fault." Holding on to her, he stared at Paige. "I didn't realize this would be a theme park ride. You okay?"

Was she?

Her mouth was dry.

Her heart rate had doubled. Maybe tripled.

She forced a nod because otherwise, she might ask him to keep his arm around her. Heaven help her, but she wanted to nestle against him.

Cuddle.

Paige gulped.

Concern clouded his eyes. "Sure?"

Okay, she needed to say something. "Positive."

Wes let go of her, and she immediately missed his warmth.

But she wouldn't complain. He was giving her a perfect day, one straight out of the holiday movies she loved to watch. She might not walk away with a happy ending when tomorrow came, but she would enjoy every minute she was here.

The sleigh turned on to a busier road.

"Welcome to Hood Hamlet," Wes said.

She forced her attention to the street in front of her.

Gasped.

Talk about quaint. Charming shops, restaurants, and cafes lined Main Street. People strolled along the wooden sidewalks. A garland hung across the road with a wreath hanging in the center. Red and white lights turned the old-fashioned lampposts into candy canes. Lights, garlands, or wreaths decorated each storefront. Sometimes all three.

Every Christmas wish—a few that Paige hadn't realized she'd made—had suddenly come true. She heated from the inside out as if she'd drunk liquid sunshine.

She glanced at Wes. "I'm in love."

Surprise flashed in his eyes.

"With Hood Hamlet," she added.

"Many feel the same way the first time they see Main Street."

Physically, they sat close together, but Paige sensed a distance between them. She wanted to bridge the gap.

She wet her lips. "Thank you for inviting me."

He stared at her before breaking eye contact. "You're welcome."

The sleigh stopped in front of the Hood Hamlet Brewing Company. Wes got out first.

Looking oh-so-handsome in his parka, scarf, and hat, Wes extended his gloved hand.

She grabbed hold. Her boots hit the hard-packed snow.

He led her to the sidewalk and let go of her hand. "Ready?"

Paige nodded. Anticipation surged through her. "I can't wait to see what this Christmas Magic celebration is all about."

Chapter Seven

Hood Hamlet locals discussed Christmas magic as openly as the weather forecast, no matter the time of year. The idea might sound woo-woo, but the number of visitors in town for the celebration suggested many believed.

Wes had never formed an opinion. Not when mountain rescuers had succeeded against the odds during daring and dangerous rescues. Not when he'd come here last December to rest and suddenly felt better than he had in months. Not even earlier this morning when he and Paige watched works of art being created during the snow sculpture contest.

What convinced him Christmas magic existed was…

Paige.

Turned out the oh-so-serious doctor was a Christmas-loving fanatic. Watching her excitement was as much fun as participating in the festivities. She was the reason for high holiday-movie ratings and decorations going up before Thanksgiving.

Bet she'd decked her condo's halls for the holidays.

"Best day ever." Standing next to him in line at the corner of Main and First, she bounced from foot to foot. Her pink cheeks and twinkling eyes complemented her wide smile. "I can see why you want to live here permanently."

"The town isn't always jam-packed like today," Wes explained, noticing how Craig hung back in the crowd. The bodyguard had been waiting when the sleigh arrived at the brewery. "But it's a great place."

"The best," the Hood Hamlet city manager said, roasting chestnuts they and people in the line behind them had ordered.

"Hood Hamlet and Christmas will be linked forever in my mind," Paige said. "But I can't wait to see what it's like in the springtime."

Wes pressed his lips together to keep from inviting her to visit then. Spending time with her was great. He had no idea hanging out with her would be so much fun. They got along better than he imagined, trying each of the activities and then some. But the only reason he'd asked Paige here was to help her out. This wasn't a date, even if it felt like one, nor had he expected a friendship to develop.

Though *friends* didn't seem like the right word given how much he enjoyed having her pressed against him in the sleigh. More than once, he'd reached for her hand only to jerk back as if he might be electrocuted if he touched her.

He shook away the thought. Refocused. "Spring is a great time for hiking and picnics."

The city manager, whose name escaped Wes, handed Paige a small paper bag of chestnuts. "Enjoy them, but they're hot."

"Thank you." As she moved to let the couple behind them come forward, Paige beamed. She held out the bag to him. "Try one."

"I bought them for you."

She nodded. "I want you to go first."

Based on the determined set of her jaw, Wes had a feeling she wouldn't relent. He ate one. Soft, not crunchy as he expected. Tasty. "It's good."

"My turn." She bit into hers before closing her eyes as if savoring the moment the way she had during the tasting at Welton Wines and Chocolates. After she swallowed, her eyes opened. "Yummy. I use walnuts or hazelnuts to accent dishes, but I might have to try chestnuts."

He remembered what she'd said about meals in her freezer. "I didn't think you cooked."

"I know how to cook, but sometimes heating a meal is easier." She finished the rest of her chestnut. "Maybe these will inspire me to come up with a new holiday dish."

He remembered what Paige had told him about working this Christmas.

Are you spending the holidays with your family?

No. I'm on call this year.

He should invite her to spend Christmas Eve with him. Even if he wanted to, he couldn't. She had to work. Hood Hamlet was too far from the hospital if she was called in.

A good excuse.

Wes ignored the mocking voice inside his head. "You'll find a way to use them."

She nodded. "Oh, look, the choir is about to perform."

Next to the large community Christmas tree, a group of high schoolers wore red scarves and Santa hats. They sang "Silent Night."

A thoughtful expression formed on Paige's face. "I wish I could sing like that."

"Everyone can sing."

"Not everyone can sing well." She blew out a breath that hung on the air. "Dogs howl if I try."

He laughed. "You're joking."

"Not really. I'm not tone-deaf, but I can't carry a tune."

"And here I thought you were perfect."

"Not even close, but thank you." She motioned to the coffee shop up the block. "Are you thirsty?"

Wes knew where she was going with this. Might

as well play along. "I could go for a peppermint hot chocolate."

Her eyes widened. "Me, too."

She was so easy to please. He'd confirmed the shop sold Paige's favorite. "Come on."

They made their way through the festival-goers. He bumped into her. "Sorry."

"It's crowded."

Other than a conference he'd attended this fall in Las Vegas and the mall a few nights ago, Wes hadn't been around this many people since the cancer. He fought the urge to hold her hand so he wouldn't lose her.

"Do you want another chestnut?" she asked.

"I might get bumped and drop it."

"You might, but I won't."

With her gloved hand, Paige fed him a chestnut. She was being playful. It meant nothing. But the act felt intimate. Worse, he enjoyed the feeling. His gaze met hers before dropping to her lips, so soft and pink and…

I want to kiss her.

The thought reverberated inside him. Wes wanted to kiss her more than he'd wanted to do anything for a very long time. He swallowed.

She smiled softly. "Thanks for inviting me to the celebration. I can't remember when I've had this much fun."

"Me, either." Wes ground out the words.

We can each look all we want but no touching.

He remembered what Craig had told him. *Kissing would be considered touching, right?*

"Oh, look." Paige motioned ahead. "The line is out the door at the coffee shop."

"Knowing the owner, Muffy will have twice the number of baristas working behind the counter, and it'll go fast."

He was correct. Muffy kept customers moving. Fifteen minutes later, they had their drinks—each topped with whipped cream, chocolate sauce, and sprinkles—and were listening to the choir.

Paige took a sip. "It doesn't get much better than this."

Wes could go anywhere, buy anything his heart desired, but at this moment, being in this small town with Paige with a warm drink in his hand was all he wanted.

A dab of whipped cream stuck to the tip of her nose. "Oops."

"Allow me." He wiped it off with his napkin. "Do you usually wear your drink?"

Laughter lit her eyes. "This is the second time with you."

He grinned. "That's why I asked."

"The answer is no, unless it's hot chocolate with whipped cream. Then, the odds are fifty-fifty."

"We'll have to see what happens next time."

Whoops. Had he asked her out again?

"It's on," Paige challenged.

Okay, she was game. Knowing that brought more relief than it should. Being with Paige made him feel lighter—happier. He didn't want the feeling to end.

Maybe they could go out when they returned to Portland. They didn't need a label. "Just tell me when and I'll—"

"Wes," a woman called out.

Every one of his muscles bunched. His spine went ramrod stiff. He hadn't heard that voice in over two years, but he recognized it immediately.

Craig, his features hard and his gloved hands clenched, headed toward them.

Paige touched Wes's arm. "Are you okay?"

He tried to nod but couldn't. Instead, he stood there frozen, waiting for the inevitable to happen.

Somehow with all the people at the festival, he could hear *her* footsteps getting closer.

The lump in his throat burned. He sipped his drink, but that didn't help. Still, drinking gave him something to do besides acknowledging her.

"I thought it was you." Annabelle stood next to him. "How are you, Wes?"

He had no choice but to look at her. She wore a long parka. Hair, not as blond as it once had been, stuck out from a fleece cap.

"Good. I'm good." He loosened his grip on his cup before he sent hot cocoa splashing everywhere. "I didn't know you were back in Oregon."

"I'm not."

The way she stared at him made Wes uneasy. "Still in New York?"

"Seattle." Annabelle wasn't smiling. She appeared wary. "As of three months ago. I missed the first two Christmas Magic in Hood Hamlet celebrations when I was living in Manhattan, so I decided to come this year."

Wes peered over her shoulder, but he didn't see anyone with her. "Are you here alone?"

"No."

He waited for her to offer more info, but she didn't. O-kay. "There's lots to do. You'll enjoy the tasting at Welton Wine and Chocolate."

Paige nodded. "Excellent chocolate."

Lines formed a V above Annabelle's nose. "Dr. Regis?"

"Hi," Paige said.

Annabelle's mouth dropped open. "You… The two of you are together now?"

"No." The word shot out bullet-fast from Wes's mouth. "We're not dating."

As her gaze bounced between him and Paige, Annabelle raised an eyebrow. "You're not?"

"Of course we aren't," Wes said a little too adamantly. He didn't owe Annabelle an explanation, but he wanted to explain so he didn't hurt her again. Not that who he was with should matter two years after they broke up. "Dr. Regis is fundraising, so she's here to meet the guys tonight."

Annabelle focused on Paige. "What are you raising money for?"

"A new cancer center," Paige said, taking a step backward.

Annabelle's face relaxed. "Oh, that makes sense. No offense, Dr. Regis, but I just couldn't see Wes dating his oncologist."

He expected Paige to say something, but she sipped her drink instead. She'd also put another step between them. Why?

"Are you seeing anyone?" Annabelle asked him.

"No," he said, nonchalantly.

Her gaze clouded. "And the cancer?"

"In remission."

Annabelle smiled. "I'm happy for you, Wes. Truly."

The sincerity in her voice and the way her smile reached her eyes told him she meant it. "Thanks."

"Nice work, Dr. Regis," Annabelle said.

Paige's bright smile had vanished, but the corners of her mouth turned up slightly. "I do what I can for my patients."

Except he wasn't her patient. Though in Annabelle's mind, he still was. Wes switched his hot chocolate to his left hand. This whole conversation was awkward.

"I hope you make the most of being healthy,"

Annabelle said.

"I'm trying." There was so much he wanted to say. "I—"

She raised her gloved hand. "What happened is in the past. I've moved on."

Wes nodded, taking the easy way out as he had two years ago. "Thanks."

"It was nice seeing you again, Wes." Annabelle smiled at Paige. "You, too, Dr. Regis. I hope the guys come through for you with your fundraising."

Paige stared through her eyelashes. "Thanks."

"Well, Merry Christmas." Annabelle didn't wait for a reply. She crossed the street.

Wes watched her disappear into the crowd. He should have said something—made amends. Instead, he'd allowed her to walk away as she had the first time. He blew out a breath.

Paige's piercing gaze scanned his face. "Are you okay?"

"I'm sorry." Wes didn't know what else to say.

"You have nothing to apologize for." Paige wasn't frowning, but her smile hadn't returned, either. It was as if someone had flicked a switch, draining her Christmas spirit. "You weren't expecting to see Annabelle."

That was an understatement. "She caught me off guard. I had no idea she was back in the Pacific Northwest. She always loved Hood Hamlet, which explains why she's at the celebration. I'm sorry it ruined your day."

"The day's not ruined. You only spoke to her for five minutes."

True, but in that short time, Paige's emotion had flip-flopped. The serious gleam in her eyes matched her expression. The bubbly Christmas elf-wannabe had turned into the competent physician who wanted to fix whatever was wrong with him.

Too bad she couldn't.

Today had been about Paige having fun. He'd succeeded until Annabelle showed up, but now a black cloud hung over them. The day ruined because of the specter of his ex-girlfriend.

But that made little sense. So what if he'd seen Annabelle? He and Paige weren't together. Still, something had caused the change in her. Annabelle or him or a combination.

"I see Craig," Paige said in the doctor's tone of hers he'd relied on over the years, but he hated hearing it again. Especially today. "He'll drive us to your lodge. Come on."

She led him toward his bodyguard.

"I'm okay," he said.

"Glad to hear it, but we have a big night ahead, so I want a chance to relax."

She was giving him an out. Wes would take it. "Let's go home."

* * *

In the guest room, Paige dressed for the benefit dinner. She'd been excited to wear the sparkly red cocktail dress. Now, all she felt was dread. The only place she wanted to be was home, covered with a fleece blanket in front of the TV.

If only that was an option tonight.

She zipped the back.

Spending the day at the festival with Wes had been wonderful—a dream come true. Whether or not Christmas magic had anything to do with it, she didn't care. All that mattered was having fun and being with him. When he suggested them getting together again, she hadn't been sure if her snow boots were touching the ground. A part of her thought he'd wanted to go out with her. Not as friends, but something more.

Stupid.

When Annabelle appeared, he'd gone from smiling to shell-shocked.

Paige's heart had ached for him. For a few seconds.

Until what they both said about her had left Paige hurting.

Okay, she shouldn't have taken their words so personally. Was she really surprised to hear them say or imply Wes wouldn't date someone like her? Maybe she'd thought otherwise, daydreaming their perfect Hallmark-holiday-movie day might turn into reality, but she knew better now.

Get over it, Regis.

Throwing herself a pity-party wasn't her style. The long shower with the fabulous waterfall showerhead had helped. She would do what she'd planned—meet Wes's friends so she could increase her donor pool for the future.

She caught her reflection in the mirror.

The easy updo complemented the neckline of her dress and dangling red earrings. The gold shoes accentuated her legs, making them appear longer. Oh, the beauty of high heels. These weren't as uncomfortable as most, so she called that a win.

"You may not catch a billionaire's eye, but there's a guy out there for you."

Someday, it will happen.

Not tonight, but it would.

Just smile.

Paige did. "Ugh, I look like a rabid animal."

She tried again. "Too much teeth. People will think I'm a psycho or starving."

This time, she kept her lips together. "Less is more will do."

Paige grabbed her purse and lined cape, a present from her parents, and made her way downstairs.

Wes faced the Christmas tree.

A frisson of nerves rippled through her.

Just smile.

She clutched her purse. "I hope I didn't keep you

waiting."

As he turned, his mouth dropped open. "Wow. You're stunning."

"Thank you." She took in his black suit and snowman-covered tie. "You look nice yourself."

The polite discussion wasn't as awkward as earlier, but she missed the easy-breezy conversation.

"Craig will drive us, so we don't have to worry about drinking and driving," Wes said.

"I'm not a big drinker," she admitted. "More than two, and I fall asleep."

"Lightweight," he teased.

"I am."

"Nothing wrong with that." He shifted his weight between his feet. "Ready to go?"

She nodded.

Fifteen minutes later, they entered Hood Hamlet Community Center with their toy donations through double doors decorated with lighted garland. A pretty woman with blond hair sat behind a table.

"Welcome to the Third Annual Christmas Magic Dinner," she greeted. "I'm Carly Porter. Can I have your name, please?"

Wes stepped forward. "Wes Lockhart and guest."

Carly checked her list. Her eyes widened. "Oh, you're one of our table sponsors. Thank you for your support."

"You're welcome."

"Jake, sweetie," Carly called out. "Can you put the

donations under the tree?"

A tall, handsome man in a suit appeared through another set of doors. He took the toys from their hands and then winked at Carly. "Hey, Wes. Thanks for the donations."

"Happy to help," Wes said. "We tasted your Bah Humbug Ale today. Great job with this year's seasonal brew."

"Thanks." Jake smiled. "That was my bartender Kai's idea."

"Toys under the tree, oh-dear-husband-of-mine," Carly said playfully.

A sheepish expression flitted across Jake's face. "I can talk about beer all night."

Carly nodded, looking amused. "Which is why you donated a private beer tasting at the brewery. You'll find a table full of wonderful items up for bid in our silent auction tonight. Dinner is at seven. Dancing begins at eight."

Paige hadn't danced in over a year. "Dancing sounds fun."

"Just ignore my two left feet," Wes joked.

She winked. "As long as you ignore mine."

With a smile, Carly handed them each a table number card. "Hold on to this. You'll need them later. If you have questions, look for people wearing a snowflake lanyard. They'll help you."

Paige glanced at hers. Table five. "Thanks."

Wes showed her his slip with a five written on it.

"Let's see where we're sitting."

With his hand at the small of her back, he led her into the multipurpose room where Christmas music played.

Two steps inside, she stopped. Gasped in delight.

Fairy lights, snowflakes, and white tulle covered the walls. Flocked trees with thick red ribbon woven around the branches and covered with silver bells and star-shaped ornaments were set around the room. Silver stars and snowflakes hung from the ceiling.

"This is gorgeous." She surveyed the space. Not an inch had been left undecorated. "I wonder if they use the same theme every year."

A beautiful woman with brown hair and a snowflake lanyard came up. "We use a similar theme, but add something new each year. The bells are the addition tonight."

Paige thought of the bell ornaments at the children's hospital. "It's beautiful."

"Thank you." The woman extended her arm. "I'm Leanne Welton. My husband, Christian, and I chair the Christmas Magic in Hood Hamlet committee."

Paige shook the woman's hand. "Paige Regis."

"Wes Lockhart," he said. "Your husband owns the wine and chocolate store."

"He and his cousin Owen do," Leanne said. "Christian and I are also with Hood Hamlet Fire and Rescue, which is how we got involved with this a couple of years ago."

"You're a member of OMSAR, too," Wes added.

"I am." Leanne studied his face. "You live at Hamlet Heights number eight."

"Good memory."

She shrugged. "It's a small town."

"A charming one," Paige said.

Wes nodded. "She hasn't been to Hood Hamlet before."

"I hope you're enjoying yourself," Leanne said.

"I am." If everyone was as friendly as Carly and Leanne, tonight might be fun. "I'm looking forward to tonight."

"Enjoy the evening." Leanne motioned to the round tables covered with white linens, silver toppers, and pretty centerpieces with flowers, eight silver stars, a table number written in silver, and red ribbon. "Eat, drink, and be merry. Don't forget about the silent auction. The money goes to a good cause."

As she went toward table five, Paige glanced over her shoulder at Wes. "The people putting this on seem nice."

"They are," he said. "Leanne was one of the paramedics called to the lodge the first year I was sick."

He'd ended up hospitalized because of that. "Everything's behind you now."

Wes nodded, but doubt remained in his eyes.

"It's true." She touched his arm. "Don't think

about the past. Let's focus on having fun tonight."

Another nod.

Their table was located at the edge of the dance floor. Two chairs remained empty. Three couples filled the other six. The three men stood to greet them. She recognized one—Blaise Mortenson.

One man who looked vaguely familiar laughed. "You live the closest but are the last one here. I should have taken the bet."

As the other men handed over money to Blaise, whom she recognized immediately, he shrugged.

She had a feeling these guys competed against each other with everything.

"Hey," Wes said. "I wanted to make a grand entrance."

"Only Santa and I get to make grand entrances," Henry said from the other table. He wore a Christmas-inspired brocade jacket, a red damask vest, and a holly-patterned tie.

"It's introduction time," Wes announced. "There will be a quiz later."

"Should I take notes?" Paige asked.

People laughed.

"I like her already," a woman in a lovely blue dress said. The other women at the table nodded.

"Paige, I'd like to introduce you to my friends." Wes motioned to the first couple. "This is Cambria and Adam. Next, we have Selah and Kieran. Then there's Blaise and Hadley."

Paige tried to memorize faces and names. Hadley was the one in the blue dress. "It's nice to meet you."

"And now you get to meet the number one table," Henry joked.

"You're at number four," Kieran quipped.

"You already know Henry," Wes said. "His date is…"

"Running late." Henry patted the empty chair. "Bronwyn will be here shortly."

"Bronwyn," they said in unison.

"It's a family name." Henry shook his head. "As if Cambria is any better."

Adam glared at him.

Cambria laughed. "Blame my parents for that."

Wes ignored them. "Brett and Laurel are seated closest to you, then Mason and Rachael, and finally Dash and Raina."

Paige repeated the names silently. She remembered the guys, but their significant others would take some memorizing. "It's a pleasure meeting you."

"Just remember, 'hey you' or 'dude' works if you forget any of us," Dash said.

Everyone sat. Wes picked up his glass of water.

"So are you still Wes's plus-one or have you moved to date status?" Mason asked.

Wes choked and then swallowed. "Mase."

Mason held up his hands. "What? It's a valid question."

Adam sighed. "He's obsessed with the bet."

"We all are. Five hundred million—"

"It's closer to six now," Blaise corrected.

Paige had no idea what they were talking about. She sipped her water.

"Have you heard about the last-single-man-standing bet?" Cambria asked her.

"No," Paige said.

Selah rolled her eyes. "Five years ago, Adam, Wes, Mason, Kieran, Dash, and Blaise made a bet. They each put ten million dollars into a pot. Whoever is the last single man standing wins."

"Blaise beta-tested a new algorithm on the fund and profits soared." Hadley beamed with pride.

"It's winner take all," Rachael added. "But if all six marry within a year of the first person, they split the fund."

Raina's eyes twinkled. "That could happen."

Dash said nothing.

"All were single until July," Raina added, sounding emotionally invested in the bet. "Then they started falling like flies."

Dash raised a pint of beer. "Not all of us."

"Yet," Raina mumbled. "Within three months Adam, Kieran, and Mason said 'I do.' Then Blaise got married last month."

Wes frowned. "Paige doesn't care about our bet."

"What's the big deal?" Mason teased. "She's your plus-one, not your date."

His friends would make sure Paige didn't get her

hopes up about Wes. Not that she would after earlier, but still… She swallowed a laugh. "No wonder you want Wes and Dash to get married."

"They want their share of the fund," Wes said.

Kieran shook his head. "We want our single friends to be as happy as we are."

The married men at the table agreed.

Wes rolled his eyes. Dash took another sip of beer.

"So winning the bet must be why you don't want to date," she said lightheartedly.

Wes's forehead creased. "I never said that."

"But it totally is the reason." Mason grinned.

The ribbing reminded Paige of her and her brother. She was happy Wes had this group of friends. Not everyone was as lucky.

"The silent auction tables are open," the DJ announced. "Remember, we're raising money for Oregon Mountain Search and Rescue. Be sure to place your bids and keep raising them."

All eight men stood at the same time. Everyone except Paige received a kiss from their husband or date.

Plus-one. Plus-one. Plus-one.

That didn't help.

"I'll be back in a few minutes," Wes said to her.

As they headed toward the silent auction tables along the far wall, Cambria sighed. "Can I just tell Henry to outbid everything?"

Laurel shook her head. "I wish you could, but

Brett's cut him off from donations until the new year."

"At least the money is for a good cause," Hadley said.

Raina leaned forward, appearing to take in what the others said.

"Is something wrong?" Paige asked.

"The guys turn everything into a competition, which means they'll try to outdo each other to win," Selah explained. "It's wonderful for the organization benefiting from the auction, but…"

Rachael shook her head. "It'll get ugly."

Paige wanted to put the women at ease. "As long as the police aren't called, no big deal, right?"

Laurel glanced around. "I'm guessing some of Hood Hamlet's finest are here tonight so…"

"Let's not worry about the guys. They're big boys with plenty of money to burn. We can rein them in if need be. I'd rather get to know Paige better." Hadley smiled. "Why don't you tell us about yourself and Wes?"

As the six women stared at Paige, she bit the inside of her cheek. "Well, there's not much to tell. He needed a plus-one tonight. And here I am."

Based on the curiosity on the others' faces, Paige didn't know if her answer would satisfy them or not. She forced herself not to gulp.

Just smile.

So she did.

Chapter Eight

Standing at the silent auction table, Wes read the description of the private wine and chocolate tasting for sixteen offered by Welton Wines and Chocolates. All of them could go. Henry could bring a date and Wes…

He forced himself not to look at Paige. He'd been fighting the urge since he left her at the table. Instead, he wrote his name, number, and bid amount on the form.

And so it begins.

The battle for this item might end up being between him, Blaise, and Dash. That wouldn't be so bad. The other guys appeared to be battling it out elsewhere.

On the far end of the auction item display,

Kieran, Adam, Brett, and Mason argued over the private brewery tasting while Henry refereed. Well, if sipping champagne and rolling his eyes counted as refereeing. Guess Brett was serious about Henry not donating more money. Wes wondered what the guy would do to get back at Brett for cutting him off during the holidays.

"The doctor cleans up nicely." Blaise took the pen from Wes's hand and upped the bid. "She's not how I remember."

The red dress. Sexy hairstyle. Those gold shoes.

Paige was so stunning she'd rendered Wes speechless when he'd seen her for the first time earlier. Probably why he wanted to keep glancing her way. "She's not at work, so she doesn't need to be serious and professional."

Blaise set the pen on the table. "How did spending the day together go?"

"Great." Smiling, Wes remembered their morning. He grabbed the pen and wrote a higher bid on the sheet. If only things had kept going so well. "Until Annabelle showed up this afternoon."

Blaise's mouth gaped. "She's back?"

"Seattle."

"Still too close." Blaise rubbed his chin. He started to speak but then stopped himself. He opened his mouth again. "What are you going to do?"

"Nothing."

"But she—"

"Annabelle has moved on." Wes glanced around to make sure no one was listening. At least that was what she'd said to him so he would take her at face value. "So have I."

Given how he reacted today, maybe he hadn't moved on as much as he'd hoped.

Blaise shook his head. "You're a bigger man than me."

No, Wes wasn't. If he were, he would have told his friends the truth over two years ago. He would have apologized to Annabelle, who had guts approaching him today. If he'd seen her first, he would have walked away.

Shame burned in his gut.

Wes Lockhart was a fraud.

The guys looked up to him like a big brother—all-knowing, responsible, brave, honest. He was none of those things.

If he were, he wouldn't have let Annabelle take the blame. He also wouldn't have been such a jerk to Blaise after he admitted having junkies for parents. But guilt had driven Wes to act that way because he'd kept a secret from everyone, too. Yet, even now, he couldn't say anything. But he needed to make sure no one discussed this, especially in front of Paige. "Please don't mention it tonight."

"I won't. That would ruin the evening." Blaise's gaze flicked to their table. The way his face brightened suggested he'd made eye contact with his wife. "So you and the lovely doctor…"

"Nothing is going on," Wes answered quickly.

"You sure about that?"

"Yes."

Blaise smirked. "Interesting, because she keeps glancing your way."

Wes moved his head slightly, but he couldn't see her.

Blaise laughed. "It won't kill you to look at her."

It might. Wes shrugged because he had no idea what he was feeling about her. He upset—hurt—her this afternoon. He wanted to make up for that tonight. Which brought him back to why she was here in the first place.

He raised his chin. "I invited Paige to this dinner for a reason. I want her to get to know you guys. She'll need more benefactors if there are cost overruns with the cancer center. Henry says it will happen, and if he and I aren't liquid—"

"I'm in," Blaise said with no hesitation.

"For what?" Dash snagged the pen and outbid Wes.

"Paige might need donations for a cancer center," Blaise said as if all she needed was to borrow a cup of sugar or an egg.

"Count me in." Dash held on to the pen. His brows furrowed. "Should I give her my contact info or will you?"

"I'll take care of it. Thanks." Wes loved these

guys. The best friends—brothers by choice—he could ask for. He didn't know what he'd do without them. Which was why he hadn't told them the truth about Annabelle. They would have been all over him. Being told he'd grown up in poverty with addicts as Blaise had was one thing. Lying about a breakup and allowing everyone to blame an innocent person was something else.

Blaise swiped the pen from Dash. He bid again.

It would be a long evening. Wes shook his head, wondering how out of hand the bidding would get. He hadn't been to one of these events in over two—almost three—years. For all he knew, the competitiveness had intensified. That gave him an idea. "Instead of trying to one-up each other, we could each pick an item to bid on."

Dash made a sour face. "Dude, where's the fun in that?"

Blaise snickered. "I agree with Wonderkid. That wouldn't be fun. It's not about what we win. It's beating you two that matters."

Dash tilted his head toward Blaise. "What he said."

It looked as if nothing had changed since the last time Wes had been at one of these with them. He snatched the pen and made a new bid. "Fine. But you suckers will lose."

"In your dreams," Dash said.

Blaise nodded. "You're going down, Lockhart."

Satisfaction flowed through Wes. They were treating him like an equal. Not someone who was sick. That made him feel great. Normal. One of them again.

"What's the deal with you and the doctor?" Dash asked, trying to snag the pen from Wes. "Is it serious?"

"We're not dating." Wes's jaw tensed. "So there's nothing to be serious about."

"But she likes you," Dash said.

"How would you know that?" Wes asked.

Dash glanced at the table where Paige sat. "Raina told me she could tell Paige did. Do you like her?"

Wes stared in disbelief. He scratched his neck. "What are you, twelve?"

Blaise laughed. "That's Henry and Mason. Dash is at least thirteen."

Dash scowled. "Twenty-eight, since you both seemed to have forgotten."

"As much as I'm enjoying this, my lovely bride is motioning me to the table." Blaise eyed the pen in Wes's hand. "This isn't over."

"No bidding during dinner or our dates might feel ignored." Dash might be the youngest, but he was skilled at keeping the peace. "We can bid after dessert. Let others run up the amount more."

None of them were looking for a bargain buy tonight.

At the far end of the silent auction, the four guys

still fought over the brewery tasting bid sheet. Henry must have given up refereeing because he was no longer there.

Dash watched Blaise head to his table. "So I heard a rumor about WEL making an acquisition."

Interesting. No one was supposed to know about the talks with NanoNeu. "WEL is always looking for new assets."

Dash laughed. "Which means you're not going to tell me anything."

"They don't call you one of the smartest men in the world for nothing, Wonderkid," Wes teased.

After Dash walked away, Wes set the pen on the table. This left him with the high bid for now.

He took his seat next to Paige. "Enjoying yourself?"

She nodded. "Did you bid on anything?"

"Yes." He glanced at his friends, who sat close to their wives or dates, heads together, talking. He went to put his arm around the back of her chair but stopped himself. "Though Blaise and Dash want it, too."

A smile tugged at Paige's lips. "I heard about the auction bidding wars."

Wes wondered what else she'd been told. Not that any knew his secrets. He'd mentioned taking a break from dating with Hadley, a professional matchmaker, when Blaise hired her so he could win the last-single-man-standing bet, but that was it. "The money goes to a good cause."

"As long as you have fun, and there's no bloodshed."

"There never is." And then Wes remembered. "Well, except for one time, but that resulted from too much bourbon and a chair Mason didn't know was behind him."

Paige laughed.

Man, Wes could get used to hearing that sound.

"Thank you for introducing me to your friends outside of the hospital," she said. "Some people act differently there. Everyone is relaxed tonight."

"Except Dash." Wes grinned. "He's the same wherever he is, which is why one of his nicknames is Mr. Status Quo."

"Does Raina know that?" Paige asked.

"She should." Wes glanced at the other table where the couple sat. Henry didn't see the two lasting, but Raina seemed good for Dash. "He's a gamer but only with video games, not with other people's feelings."

Servers dressed in black carried salad plates and baskets of bread. Another filled wine glasses with red or white wine. The bottles came from Welton Wineries.

Wes sipped the Cabernet Sauvignon. Full-bodied and dry.

Salad and rolls were served first. The main entrees followed. Wes appreciated how his friends included

Paige in the conversation. She smiled more than she had earlier. That pleased him.

Paige took a bite of the salmon. "This is delicious. How is your steak?"

"Great."

Servers removed the dishes and utensils from the table. They refilled wine glasses. As his friends spoke about everything from the NASDAQ to the shows on the latest entry into the streaming market, Paige held her own. Doing so wasn't easy with so many strong personalities—male and female—at the table. He was impressed.

Dessert plates with slices of Bûche de Noel were set in front of them. The Yule log chocolate cake was mouthwatering good.

"I didn't think I could eat another bite," Paige said in a low voice. "But I can't let this go to waste."

"Go for it."

After savoring the first bite, Paige dug in. Her smile told him how much she enjoyed the dessert. She wasn't as carefree as she'd been this morning, but she didn't appear as closed-off as this afternoon.

Progress.

Maybe he could get her to open up more.

He leaned closer to her. "Easier to eat the whipped cream when it's part of the cake and not hot cocoa?"

"Much easier." As laughter filled her eyes, she raised her chin. "None on my face this time."

Except Wes missed seeing a dollop on her lip or a dab on her nose. "Good job."

"Now that dinner's over, it's time to boogie," the DJ announced. "Grab a partner and join us on the dance floor."

Everyone rose from the table, including Henry and his date, Bronwyn, who had shown up in the middle of dinner. That left Wes and Paige alone.

"Would you like to dance?" he asked.

"Sure." Paige sounded indifferent, but she hadn't said no.

Wes led her to the dance floor. The beat was fast. As people waved their arms in the air, they moved to the music. He enjoyed watching Paige.

Two songs later, the music slowed. Couples went into each other's arms.

Wes's pulse picked up. "Want to keep dancing?"

She nodded.

Again, not the most enthusiastic response, but he would take it.

He placed one hand around her and clasped his free hand with hers. Her skin was warm and soft. No gloves to get in the way of the skin-on-skin contact.

His friends danced with their wives and dates, exchanging kisses and staring into each other's eyes. Wes hadn't done that with a woman since Annabelle. He missed the closeness, but he kept his distance from Paige. That was for the best.

Still, moving around the dance floor with her felt

right. Natural. That would be enough.

It had to be.

She glanced over his shoulder. "I didn't know what to expect from a small-town event, but everything has been wonderful."

"I'm impressed with the Christmas Magic celebration," he admitted. "I'm glad this happens annually."

"I want to come back next year."

"Me, too."

But a question lingered. Given the silence, he wondered if she was thinking the same thing as him.

Who would be with Paige next year?

Wes didn't want to think about it. "I'm happy you're here today with me."

"Me, too." Paige grinned, not the closed-mouth smile, but a full-on one with teeth. "Thanks for the invitation."

"Wes!" Mason shouted before pointing to the ceiling. "Look up."

A ball of mistletoe hung from a red ribbon.

Uh-oh. Wes's heart plummeted to his feet.

Paige stiffened.

Things were going well with her tonight. He didn't want anything to ruin it.

Henry swirled his date until he stood next to them. "You'd better kiss, or you'll have bad luck in the new year."

"Kiss, kiss, kiss," Adam and Kieran chanted.

Dash made a smacking sound with his lips.

Wes rolled his eyes. By egging him on, his friends were once again proving, despite their billions, they were teenagers in men's bodies. He got it. This was what they did, juvenile or not. But he hated putting Paige on the spot. "We don't have to kiss."

She shrugged. "It's tradition. And who wants a year of bad luck?"

He didn't. "If you're game…"

Something flickered in her eyes but disappeared before he could decipher it. "I am."

That was the only invitation he needed.

Wes lowered his mouth to hers. He would make this brief. A brush of his lips. A peck.

At the moment of contact, something sparked between them, shooting through him to the tips of his toes.

What was that? A static shock?

He might have cared more about the questions if he hadn't realized they were kissing.

Her lips were soft and warm. She tasted sweet with a hint of chocolate—the cake. Wanting more, he pressed his mouth harder against hers, his arm around her waist, pulling her closer to him.

She went eagerly, cutting the distance between them in half.

Wes's fingers on his free hand laced with Paige's—tightened. His mouth moved over hers, exploring and tasting.

This.

This is what I've been missing.

Not only when he was sick.

But his entire life.

Paige's kiss rocked him to his core. Nothing had ever felt like this.

Warning bells sounded in his head.

He ignored them.

He wanted to soak up all of her and her kiss…

Common sense shouted to back away now.

He didn't.

Couldn't.

Paige was everything Wes hadn't known he needed, and he didn't want to let her go.

* * *

Wes was kissing her. Under the mistletoe, and only to ward off bad luck, but it was still a kiss.

A fantastic one.

The best one ever?

She'd need more to know for sure.

As his lips moved over hers, Paige arched against him, wanting to bridge what small space remained between them. She tasted a tantalizing combination of heat, salt, and chocolate that had her wanting more.

Just a mistletoe kiss.

Logically, she knew that.

A holiday tradition.

She knew that, too.

They were only playing along.

Nothing more.

But kissing him was like…magic.

Pleasurable sensations pulsed through Paige. She relished each tingle, every chill, losing herself in the moment.

In him.

She splayed her hand, the fabric of his jacket brushing against her palm.

Solid and strong.

A moan sounded.

She froze.

Wait. Was that her?

Heat flooded her face.

What was she doing?

Paige jerked back, but she didn't get far with Wes's arm around her.

Her lips no longer touched Wes's, but their faces were close. Not quite kissing distance, but if she moved forward an inch…

He stared at her. His breathing appeared to be as ragged as hers.

His friends clapped and cheered.

Ugh. This was one side of his friends she didn't appreciate. Given Wes's frown, he likely agreed.

"Some kiss," Blaise said.

Mason laughed. "Plus-one for the win."

"And my streak continues." Henry beamed.

Paige's cheeks burned. She forced herself not to cringe or hunch her shoulders. Standing in the center of the dance floor left her no place to hide from the curious stares of strangers or people she hardly knew. Her muscles tensed. She struggled against the fight-or-flight instinct trying to take over.

She was used to being in front of other doctors or speaking at medical conferences, but that was different. She hated this kind of attention. And she didn't appreciate others turning something so personal—so precious and intimate—into a joke with her and Wes as the punchline.

Not right.

Especially when she had no idea what had happened.

It was a kiss.

Just a kiss.

Except the kiss felt like so much more.

Did he feel the same way as her? Or was he thinking about Annabelle?

That thought doused Paige like a bucket of ice water.

His and his ex-girlfriend's words from earlier pounded in her head. That told Paige exactly what this kiss meant to him.

N-O-T-H-I-N-G.

Time to regain control and forget the kiss.

Tomorrow she could forget him.

Paige inhaled, hoping to slow her heart rate and

pulse, but all she got was a whiff of Wes's scent, tickling her nose and making her want another kiss.

Ugh.

This was so not good.

"Kudos," Henry said. "Now get out of the way so others can try to up your silver screen romantic kiss."

She was happy to step aside, so she shrugged out of Wes's grasp to let Brett and Laurel take their place under the mistletoe.

Guess that was the popular spot tonight.

Paige wasn't one for regrets, but a part of her wished she hadn't kissed Wes. She had a feeling all future kisses would be judged against his.

"Let's sit." Wes sounded calm as if the kiss had been no big deal, when he'd redefined her definition of a kiss.

Paige followed him. He pulled out her chair, and she sat.

Wes rubbed the back of his neck. He started to speak but then pressed his lips together.

Something was going on with him. The kiss or maybe Annabelle. Paige might as well ask. "You okay?"

"I'll get us drinks." He didn't answer her question, so either he was avoiding it or he could be thirsty. "What would you like?"

"Ginger ale." She'd only had one glass of Chardonnay with dinner, but that was enough.

Especially around Wes, who'd left her nerve

endings dancing and her lips begging for more kisses.

Stupid.

Applause sounded.

With big grins on their faces and their eyes full of hearts, Brett and Laurel stepped aside.

Blaise and Hadley took their place under the mistletoe.

Kissing Wes didn't mean anything.

Paige repeated the phrase. Maybe it didn't, but she'd kissed boyfriends and dates. No one had ever kissed her the way Wes had.

Made her feel so treasured and alive.

Her crush suddenly felt like a frustrating annoyance. One she wanted to move on from and forget about ASAP.

Wes set her drink and a pint of beer on the table before sitting. He picked up his glass and took a sip.

Her hands trembled, so she didn't trust herself with a full glass yet. Spilling all over herself wasn't how she wanted to end the evening. She flexed her fingers.

"Thanks for playing along," he said finally.

Did that mean he didn't think the kiss was out-of-this-world? Of course it did. She forced a smile, one she hoped appeared nonchalant, which was the exact opposite of how she felt discussing what happened on the dance floor.

"It's a Christmastime tradition." Somehow, she kept her voice even and free of emotion. The steadiness surprised her.

He nodded.

"You're a good kisser, too." Oops, she hadn't meant to say that.

"Thanks." Wes smiled, almost shyly, which was unexpected. "You are, too."

So this wasn't awkward. At least, he hadn't thought the kiss sucked. "Thanks."

Which was how he'd replied, but she didn't know what else to say.

"I should have asked Jim and Nora to hang mistletoe at the lodge."

Paige wasn't about to think that meant he wanted to kiss her again. Her hopes—however a longshot they might be—had been dashed this afternoon. "There's time before Christmas."

Wes's gaze met hers. "I meant for…tonight. For us."

Oh. Anticipation rocketed through Paige. She shouldn't be so excited, but she wiggled her toes. Guess he liked the kiss as much as she did. That was a good thing. It had to be.

"We're both smart," she said. "We can figure something out if you want."

He raised an eyebrow. "You think?"

She nodded, not feeling as certain as she acted, but being in the medical field had allowed her to hone that skill.

"Dude." Dash clapped Wes on the back. "We

need to bid. Some guy named Sean Hughes outbid us."

"Sean owns Hughes Snowboard, a local manufacturer with a store on Main Street," Wes explained. "He's a mountain rescue volunteer."

"Good for him, but one of us needs to win." Dash sounded outraged.

Wes appeared ready to laugh, but somehow held himself together. "Go show him no one messes with our bidding."

"Come with me," Dash pressed. "So you can outbid me. Or I can let you go first since you're the old man of the group."

"Very funny, kiddo," Wes said, dryly.

"Do you mind if he leaves you for a few minutes?" Dash asked her."

Wes glanced at Paige, who saw the question in his eyes. For some reason, he appeared to want her permission, which was sweet but unnecessary.

"Go ahead," she encouraged. The bidding war was a time-honored tradition between the guys. From what she'd heard earlier, this was Wes's first fundraising event since his diagnosis. "I need to figure out my wish."

"Wish?"

She motioned to the stars in the centerpiece. "Each is an ornament with a slot in the back. Everyone at the dinner is supposed to write a Christmas wish on their table number card, stick it into a star, and take it home."

He glanced from her to the stars. "Why didn't I know that?"

"I didn't know, either," Dash said.

She smiled at them. "People with the snowflake lanyards visited each table while you guys were at the silent auction."

"Oh." Dash grinned. "We were too preoccupied to care. That's what happens at auctions."

Not just at auctions, but Paige kept her smile in check. "I have a feeling you might lose sight of a few things whenever you're together."

"Guilty as charged," Dash admitted. "Let's go."

"Think of a good wish." Wes kissed her forehead. "I'll be back soon."

Paige watched him go and then stared at the closest star ornament. She knew what she wanted, but Wes was making her long for something…more. Should she waste a wish if it had no chance of coming true?

Chapter Nine

After placing his final bid, Wes returned to the table. He hadn't wanted to leave Paige earlier, but she'd seemed to want him to go with Dash. For the best. Wes might have kissed her again had he stayed. But they had plenty of time after the dinner ended. Casual kisses with or without mistletoe sounded good to him. He hoped she agreed.

Until they were alone later, Wes would be on his best behavior around his friends, who watched him with sly glances and lopsided grins. That told him he might have gotten carried away kissing Paige.

He had.

And would do it again.

So sue him.

If Wes could package the tingles he'd felt with her

lips against his, he would make another billion. He couldn't wait for more kisses, but giving the guys more ammunition wasn't happening.

Oh, he could take it, but Paige had been uncomfortable when his friends pointed out the mistletoe and the ribbing ensued. He didn't want her feeling that way again.

She stared up at him. "Do you think you'll win the tasting?"

"I gave it my best shot, but Dash is determined to walk home with it, and so is Blaise." Wes had made a final bid before walking away, not caring what his friends did. He would rather spend the rest of the evening with Paige. "No matter who wins, OMSAR will be happy with the money, and all of us will be included when the tasting happens."

Paige was part of the "all," but he wasn't ready to say that to her right now. Soon, though.

As the DJ played a popular song, she swayed to the music. That gave Wes an idea. If kissing had to wait, he could think of an alternative. He extended his arm. "May I have this dance?"

"I'd love to dance again." Eyes twinkling, Paige took his hand, lacing her fingers with his—a simple gesture but one he could get used to easily—and stood.

A new song played and then another. At wedding receptions—three during the past five months—Wes couldn't remember dancing so much or having as much fun.

Champagne bottles popped.

"Ladies and gentlemen," the DJ announced. "That's the signal the night is coming to a close. This is the final song."

When the music stopped, they returned to their table and sat. Servers passed out champagne-filled flutes. Wes took two and handed one to Paige. Her face was flushed from dancing. A silver star ornament was in front of her. He must have missed that on the table before.

"Is your wish inside the star?" he asked.

Staring at the ornament, her gaze softened. "Yes."

"What did you wish for?" he asked.

Paige's forehead creased. "If you tell someone, it won't come true."

"You told me about the twenty-five million," he reminded.

"I thought you were Santa."

He had a solution. "Picture me with a beard, glasses, hat, suit, and boots."

Paige studied him before shaking her head. "I can't."

Her expression made him laugh. "Okay, you don't have to tell me."

She motioned to the centerpiece where one star remained. "You haven't made your wish."

Wes hadn't. He didn't need to. His money could make any wish come true except for…

"You thought of one," she said as if reading his mind.

His lips parted. "How did you know?"

"Your expression changed." Perceptive, but her medical training could have taught her that. She pushed his table number card and a pen toward him. "Have at it. I won't peek."

Wes scribbled *Remain healthy*. Money couldn't buy him that. As he set the pen on the table, something else came to him.

Love.

A word as clear as if someone had spoken. Only this was inside his head.

Where did that come from?

His imagination. Either that or he'd had one too many drinks. That made the most sense because that was the last thing he wanted. He dropped the pen onto the table.

"Finished?" she asked.

Wes focused on the card. No reason to look anywhere else—at *anyone* else.

Nope. What he wrote was a great Christmas wish. He needed nothing more. "Yes."

"Fold the card and put it inside the star," she instructed.

He did, removed the last star from the centerpiece, and stuck the paper into the back.

Done.

Except it didn't feel finished.

"Now, you can hang the star on your tree."

Maybe once he was home, he'd get his head where it needed to be.

"And now, a final word before we say goodnight," the DJ said.

Bill Paulson, a firefighter and mountain rescuer who Wes had gotten to know over the years, held a microphone in one hand and a flute filled with bubbly in the other.

"That's my Billy," a middle-aged woman said from a nearby table.

"Hey, Mom," Bill called out.

The crowd laughed, and the woman grinned.

"I want to thank our chairpersons for tonight. This is the third year that Leanne and Christian Welton have run the event, and each Christmas Magic in Hood Hamlet celebration keeps getting better." Bill raised his glass. "Thanks for the magical day, and good luck next year."

As people cheered, Bill drank.

Paige tapped her glass against Wes's. Despite the noise in the room, the chime hung in the air. "I wonder what they'll add."

She took a sip.

So did Wes.

Seeing her happy pleased him. He leaned closer, putting his arm around the back of her chair. "My guess is candy canes."

She tilted her head as if pondering the idea. "I

could see that."

Instead of lowering his arm, he kept it around her. Scooting closer would be nice, but not with the way Blaise was eyeing him with curiosity.

Bill raised his glass again. "I also want to acknowledge our sponsors: Welton Winery, Welton Wines and Chocolates, Hood Hamlet Flowers, Hughes Snowboards, and the Mount Hood Brewing Company. Today, and especially this dinner, happened because of their support."

The crowd applauded.

"And a final thanks to all of you," Bill said sincerely. "For being here and bidding on the great auction items. We couldn't pull this off without you. Oregon Mountain Search and Rescue and Hood Hamlet Fire and Rescue appreciate your support."

The crowd cheered. A few people whistled.

Bill blew a kiss to a pregnant blonde who smiled at him. "Don't forget to write your Christmas wish on the card with your table number and place it in a star from the centerpieces. Please take it with you when you leave. A favor you can hang on your tree at home as a thank you from OMSAR and Hood Hamlet Fire and Rescue. Remember, we're celebrating Christmas magic today, so it's okay to make a big wish."

People laughed.

"Wish big or go home," someone yelled.

Paige picked up her star. "Guess I made the right wish."

Wes wondered what she'd wished for—a cure for cancer?

"Goodnight, everybody," Bill said. "Drive safe, and we'll see you next year."

Guests rose from tables. Some stood around. Others headed to the exit. Dash and Mason went to pay for the items they won.

"After-party at my place. I have food, drinks, and mistletoe!" Henry shouted over the crowd and then shot a pointed look at Wes. "Thanks to Laurel's mad holiday decorating skills, I'm calling the place the Mistletoe Lodge from Black Friday until Epiphany."

Both Laurel and Brett shook their heads, but Henry would expect no less from his friends and parents of his goddaughter.

"If you're staying with Wes, park there, and rides will be provided," Henry added, which meant the alcohol would be flowing. "Lots of fun still ahead of us."

"We don't have to stay long," Wes whispered to Paige. He would rather go home, but she was there to get to know people. She'd spoken to Adam, Kieran, and Blaise, who'd already offered his help, during dinner. "But this will give you the chance to get to know Brett, Mason, and Dash better. Given Henry's past parties, everyone might not make it to the brunch tomorrow."

"That's fine." Paige ran her fingers along the edge of the star. "I know why I'm here."

Wes didn't like how her smile had disappeared. "You're here to have fun."

"And find benefactors." She continued studying the star.

Using his finger, he raised her chin, so she was looking at him. "It's called mixing business with pleasure. Emphasis on the pleasure."

Her lips curved upward.

That was better. "Ready to see what Henry has in store for us?"

Paige raised a brow. "That sounds ominous."

Wes laughed. "With Henry, you never know. But one thing is for certain, we won't be bored."

* * *

Henry's lodge was slightly smaller than Wes's, but the feel was similar except for the number of Christmas trees and decorations. Christmas carols played from hidden speakers. The scents of pine and cinnamon filled the air.

Paige stared in awe. "This is better than the hospital and dinner combined."

"Henry does nothing halfway," Wes explained.

Laurel nodded. "Henry made me add more after I finished. He said the house wasn't Christmassy enough."

Paige stared at a moving display of elves and snowmen in the entryway. Not even holiday movies went this far. The décor was over-the-top yet still tasteful. Laurel had done an excellent job. "I hope he's pleased now."

"He is, but the mistletoe was all him." Laurel blew out a breath. "Frank helped him hang it."

"Henry's calling this place Mistletoe Lodge," Wes said.

"I heard that." Laurel rolled her eyes. "Please don't encourage him, or I'm afraid of what he might attempt next year."

They stepped into the great room to find mistletoe sprigs hanging from the ceiling. Dozens.

"I've never seen this much mistletoe in my life. Is there any room without it?" Paige asked.

"The bathrooms, but I haven't checked each yet." Laurel rubbed her forehead. "Henry means well, but the mistletoe is his way of pushing the unmarried couples together."

"Dash and Raina."

"You and Wes, too."

Paige stiffened. "We're not…"

Wes touched her shoulder. "He can't think mistletoe will make a difference."

"Henry only sees the possibilities," Laurel explained. "It's both a strength and a flaw of his. But he's the reason Brett and I are together and have Noelle so maybe we shouldn't try holding Henry back."

"Holding him back?" Paige asked, not

understanding.

"I asked Frank to remove half of the mistletoe they'd put up," Laurel admitted.

Wes laughed. "Typical Henry."

Paige looked up. Mistletoe hung every three feet. A serpentine path was required to avoid it. If there had been more… "Green sprigs must have covered the entire ceiling."

Laurel nodded. "It looked festive."

Paige grinned. "Guess that's one way to make sure people kiss."

"Friends." Henry stood by a gorgeous ten-foot-tall Christmas tree and clapped. "It's time for presents."

"Presents?" Raina asked.

Henry nodded. "Christmas requires gifts."

"This should be interesting," Laurel said, before going over to stand by her husband, Brett.

"Don't open yours until I say go." Henry handed each person a large box decorated in cute Santa-patterned wrapping paper with elaborate bows on top. He picked up the one he'd set aside. "There's even a present for me."

The gift tag on Paige's had her name written on it, but she had no idea what to expect. None of her friends gave out gifts like this. Okay, Henry was known for being eccentric, and he had billions, but still…

"Henry considers everyone in this room, little

Noelle, and his staff, family. He likes to do things for those he cares about," Wes whispered. "Whatever the gift, no matter how extravagant or not, just smile and say thank you."

"But I'm not—"

"You're here with me, so you are tonight."

"Now on the count of three…" Henry's face lit up with excitement. "I want you to open your present. Don't wait for anyone else. One, two, three!"

Paige glanced at Wes, who was ripping the paper off his gift.

When in Rome…

She did the same and then lifted the lid off the box. White tissue paper came next, so she pushed that aside. Underneath were a pair of monogrammed snowmen-covered flannel pajamas and matching slippers.

Paige ran her fingertips along the soft fabric. "These are cute."

"We match." Wes held up his. "Well, except for the W and the P."

"Thanks so much, Henry," she said to him.

People spoke over each other to thank him and show off what they'd received.

Eyes gleaming and a satisfied smile on his face, Henry clutched Santa pajamas and watched everyone else. Bronwyn held the same pattern as Henry and kissed his cheek. Adam and Cambria had reindeer, including one with a red nose. Blaise and Hadley had the most adorable llamas on theirs. Brett and Laurel had penguins with an extra pair in a smaller size for their daughter, Dash and Raina pointed at the various gnomes on theirs. Kieran and Selah had the sweetest polar bears in hats. Mason and Rachael had gingerbread people and hearts.

"Go put on your new pajamas," Henry announced.

The couples staying there went to their bedrooms. The others lined up to use the downstairs powder room.

Wes leaned closer to Paige. "I had no idea what Henry planned for tonight, but matching Christmas pajamas never crossed my mind."

"It's sweet."

"Yes." Wes sounded a little uncertain. "We'll have to see if what comes next is as sweet."

As soon as everyone changed, Henry led them into his movie room with comfy recliner chairs with drink holders and trays. A fully stocked bar was in the corner. As people walked in, they greeted the bartender, an older gentleman named Frank, who had been mentioned earlier.

Paige sat beside Wes in the second row of seats. Christmas-themed fleeces, one per couple, were passed out.

"Tonight, we're playing movie drinking games. I have a triple feature for you." Henry wore a Santa hat with his pajamas. "The first two are short shows that originally premiered before any of us were born. The third is a full-length film. After the shorts, those who aren't staying here can go to Wes's lodge if you're tired."

Adam raised his hand. "That would be us."

"Same," Blaise added.

Wes nodded. "Me, too."

"This happens when you turn thirty," Dash quipped.

Everyone shushed him.

"Each show comes with rules which I've printed out so no one misses anything," Henry continued.

Frank placed a large poster board on an easel. Written across the top was The Grinch Who Stole Christmas Drinking Game Rules. Below it listed the times a person needed to take a drink.

Groans and laughs sounded.

Undeterred, Henry beamed. "Our first feature is a Dr. Seuss classic. The themes of loneliness, transformation, and community may resonate with some of us."

"Thank you, Professor Davenport," Mason heckled.

In the seats in front of Paige, Hadley kissed Blaise's cheek. Next to them, Laurel raised Brett's hand and kissed the top of it.

"Tonight's beverage choices include mulled wine, eggnog, Christmas Cosmos, Merry Manhattans, Bah Humbug Ale from the Hood Hamlet Brewery, Candy

Cane Shooters, and Peppermint Patty Shots."

As Paige read the first rule, her muscles tensed. "I haven't watched this since I was a kid, but I think they say the Grinch a lot."

"Take small sips." Wes leaned into her. "We can leave after the first show, okay?"

She nodded. At least the wine she'd drunk had been a while ago. "So all I need to do is make one drink last the entire show."

"You catch on fast," Dash, who sat next to her, said.

She grinned. "I have to with this crowd."

Wes laughed. "That's true, and you're doing a great job."

Feeling a rush of pride at his compliment, she straightened.

Henry cleared his throat as if to quiet people. "Pick a drink and a shot."

Paige thought Frank must be an expert at this because he had everyone served quickly. Festive Merry Christmas bowls filled with popcorn and red and green M&M's came next, one for each couple.

Wes placed his hand over hers.

Her stomach flip-flopped from his touch and seeing them wearing the same pajamas. It was silly, but she loved Henry's gift. She'd never had matching pajamas with anyone, not even her brother, unless they'd been so young she had no memory of it. She and Wes weren't a couple like the others here, but that didn't matter to her. Being with him gave her a sense of belonging Paige hadn't known she was missing. Yes, it would end shortly, but she was happy to experience the feeling tonight.

"Ready?" he asked.

"I don't suppose you mean to leave," she joked.

"Seriously, dude," Dash said. "The doc's a keeper."

"Wonderkid is correct," Mason said from the row behind them.

"Let the bet go, guys." As he focused on her, laughter lit Wes's eyes. "We'll be out of here before you know it."

And then what? Anticipating another kiss, her heart rate increased.

The lights dimmed, and the screen showed the opening title.

Paige enjoyed it and found herself teary-eyed. More than once, she caught Wes watching her. The third time she had to ask. "What?"

"Nothing," he said before looking at the screen.

When the credits rolled, she still had half of her eggnog left. Wes's bourbon had the same amount. Little sips had worked well.

Henry stood. "We'll take a ten-minute intermission so refill your drinks and be sure to grab a shot."

"Let's leave," Wes whispered.

As soon as she stood, he placed his hand at the

small of her back. "Thanks for the after-party, Henry. We'll see some of you tomorrow at eleven for brunch. If you're not there, I hope your hangovers aren't too bad."

Some guys jeered. Others laughed.

No one else rose as if they were ready to leave. Maybe they wanted to watch the other short show. Downstairs, she and Wes gathered their things.

"Craig is pulling into the garage, so there's no need to get dressed," Wes said. "Put on your cape so you don't get cold."

A few minutes later, they stood in his great room. Christmas music played, and wood crackled in the fireplace. Warmth enveloped Paige like a hug. "This place is so homey."

He glanced around "Not quite as Christmassy as Henry's lodge."

"I prefer this," she said honestly.

"Me, too." Wes hung his star on the tree. "But something is missing, so I borrowed this from Henry."

She hadn't noticed Wes carrying anything. "What?"

He pulled a sprig of green from his pocket. "Henry has so much he won't miss this at all."

Her pulse galloped. "Mistletoe."

"Mistletoe kisses are a Christmas tradition."

Standing in matching pajamas with her heart rate picking up with each passing second, she needed to know where things stood between them. Plus-one, friends, for fun, something else?

"Casual fun," he added.

Her breath hitched. That was the answer she needed. Paige couldn't deny her disappointment, but what he said wasn't unexpected. He'd been honest. The problem was her. Seeing so many happy couples at the dinner and at Henry's made Paige want that.

Not someday.

Sooner.

Now.

Knowing it wouldn't happen grated.

But that wasn't Wes's fault.

Hope filled his eyes. "Will that work for you?"

Casual. Fun.

Paige repeated the words mentally. She was up for fun, but she had to be careful. Her heart was ready for more. "I might be up for another mistletoe kiss."

Wes held the sprig over his head, leaving the next step up to her.

One kiss.

She rose on her toes and planted her lips against his. Hard. She soaked in his warmth and his taste. As his lips moved over hers, he put both arms around her. He was solid and strong and sexy.

Paige had wondered if she'd exaggerated how well he kissed. Nope. If anything, she'd understated his skills. No one had ever kissed her so thoroughly in her life.

Talk about swoon-worthy.

Thank goodness his arms were around her, or she might find herself on the floor. She lost herself in his kiss until warning bells sounded in her head.

She had no idea how long they'd been kissing but…

Enough.

Paige needed to protect herself—her heart. She drew the kiss to an end.

"Wow." His gaze locked on her. The desire in his eyes was clear. "Another win for tradition."

Not trusting her voice, she nodded. She wanted more time to calm her rapid pulse and breathing.

"We could try that again," he said.

"We could, but that wouldn't be a good idea."

His jaw jutted forward. "Why not?"

"You want casual fun."

He nodded.

Wes Lockhart was handsome, charming, and smart. He made her laugh and his generosity touched her heart. It would be so easy to give in, to do what he wanted, but Paige couldn't. That wouldn't be good for her.

She pushed back her shoulders. "I don't."

Chapter Ten

Morning came too soon for Wes. The clock read seven. Not as early as he thought, but that didn't keep him from yawning. He'd barely slept, which explained why his tired eyes burned. An hour or two more of rest would help, but he doubted sleep would come.

Not when Paige's words still played on an endless loop through his head. The way they had all night.

I don't.

Wes hadn't expected her to say that. Call him egotistical or vain, but most women he'd dated had settled for whatever he would give them. That included Annabelle.

Truth was, he'd never had to work hard to keep a relationship going. He wasn't even sure he knew how to do that, but he'd thought Paige would be the same as the women before her.

Admitting that made him sound like a big jerk. Something he'd been trying not to be. But he'd assumed wrongly about her.

I don't.

The words echoed through his brain, making him feel an odd mix of emotions—regret over not pursuing more with her and relief at not being able to hurt her.

She hadn't appeared upset. Based on the way her expression and posture relaxed, saying those two words brought her relief, too.

Wes didn't like drama, and Paige had provided none. She hadn't explained her feelings or tried to change his mind about what he wanted. Instead, she'd thanked him for a lovely evening and went upstairs to the guest room without saying another word.

He'd been tempted to follow her. He'd gotten as far as the staircase until he realized nothing he said would change anything.

And it shouldn't.

He respected Paige for not settling for less than she wanted. Even if it meant not getting what he wanted.

I don't.

Unfortunate, because spending more time with her—kissing her again—appealed to him on a gut level. But if she wasn't interested in casual and he didn't do serious, they were better off not starting anything.

Too late, a voice in his head mocked.

Wes ignored it. He hadn't invited her to Hood Hamlet for a romantic getaway. This was more him being a not-so-secret Santa, a way to help her and the cancer center.

He had to face facts. Two kisses meant nothing in the grand scheme of things. Spending a day and an evening together didn't mean much, either.

Still, a heaviness pressed against his chest.

Wes shook it off.

After the brunch, he would say goodbye to Paige. They would return to Portland and to their lives.

Separate ones.

Who knew when he'd see her again?

No big deal.

Except, the thought of not seeing her rattled him.

Weird.

Because she was just…

He wasn't sure what Paige Regis was to him.

Which told him the sooner he put this weekend behind him, the better. All he had to do was get through this morning and brunch.

Wes climbed out of bed, showered, and dressed. At this hour, everyone except Nora and Jim would be asleep. His friends slept in whenever they stayed overnight. A few might even be late to the eleven o'clock brunch, but no one cared. He wanted people to feel as if his home was their home.

On his way downstairs, he heard Christmas music playing. The festive song had a fast beat. Someone sang along, off-key but full of enthusiasm.

A smile spread across his face. Whoever was singing was enjoying herself. He went into the kitchen.

Paige stood at the island's counter, belting out a lyric about what she wanted for Christmas. Her hair was pulled back into a low ponytail. She wore a robe over her pajamas and no makeup. A smudge of flour stained her cheek.

Beautiful.

As she pressed a circle cookie cutter into rolled-out dough on a large cutting board, she sang another verse, shimmying her shoulders and bopping to the beat.

Something in Wes's chest shifted. Two tectonic plates colliding. The earth didn't shake, but his heart felt as if it skipped a beat. Okay, three.

Paige cooking in his kitchen was wholesome and sweet, yet his attraction increased exponentially, sending his temperature rising. Each nerve ending stood at alert, eager for something. He had no idea what, but if Santa was taking requests, Wes wanted Paige for Christmas.

He wet his lips.

She captivated him.

Forget hearing "I don't."

He wanted her to say "I do."

Whoa. Where had that come from?

Wes must be more tired than he realized because *that* was the last thing he needed. He had a plan where women were concerned.

No dating. No relationship. Nothing.

Time to stop mooning like a lovestruck teenager. He cleared his throat.

She glanced up, her lips parting as if surprised to see him.

"Good morning." Wes sat on the opposite side of the island as if everything was okay and he wouldn't be calling his therapist tomorrow to find out what was wrong with him. "You're up early."

"My internal alarm clock makes sleeping in difficult. It goes off at six no matter what."

He glanced in the great room. No one else was there. "Have you seen Nora?"

"She ran to the market to get more strawberries. The ones in the refrigerator had mold." Paige raised the cookie cutter. "I offered to help with brunch so she asked me to make the biscuits."

"You seem to know what you're doing."

"It's my first time, but Nora is a good teacher. She said they're hard to mess up."

"That's a strong vote of confidence."

"I know, right?" Paige washed her hands before pouring coffee into a mug and adding a dash of cream the way he liked it. She gave him the cup. "Nora also said you're not a functional human being until you drink your first coffee."

Steam rose from the cup. He sniffed the fragrant aroma. "I'm not that bad."

"I wouldn't know." Paige returned to cutting the dough and placing the circles on a baking sheet. "She said to limit conversation, or you'll get snippy. That surprised me. You don't strike me as a little ankle-biter dog. You're more of a retriever or lab."

Wes focused on the coffee. He took a sip. Hot and strong. Just what he needed. He drank more. The warm mug heated the palms of his hands.

"I'm functional now," he announced. "No snipping or barking."

Laughing, she put the sheet in the oven, closed the door, and set the timer.

Another taste and he felt nearly human. "Sleep well?"

"The bed is so comfortable, and those pillows are like sleeping on clouds." Paige rolled out a new batch of dough. "You look a little tired."

"I am." He watched as a flurry of emotions crossed her face, but seeing the concern made him want to speak up. "Before you go all doctor on me, I feel fine. I just didn't sleep well."

The set of her jaw and the lines above her nose were typical of her Dr. Regis persona. Funny, but now he almost thought of her as two different people—the oncologist and the woman.

"Do you know why?" she asked.

Saying "you" might not go over well, but he didn't want to lie. "My brain wouldn't settle."

That much was true, but she was the reason.

"It was a full day." She didn't sound convinced that was his reason. "More coffee?"

"Nora trained you well, but I have half a cup left."

"What kept your brain awake?" Paige asked.

Wes should have known she'd ask. His fault because he'd opened the door to the question. For all he knew, Paige had figured it out for herself. Might as well say it. "You."

The cookie cutter slipped from her hand and clattered against the cutting board. "Me?"

Her reaction told him she hadn't known. Interesting. "I enjoy spending time with you. Kissing you. Yet—"

"You're used to getting what you want."

It wasn't a question. "I am, but only if someone else wants that, too. That, however, didn't stop the entitled me from pouting."

She laughed. "Pouting?"

"As much as a thirty-five-year-old man can pout when he's disappointed."

"I'm… I'm not sorry for how I feel."

"I don't need an apology."

Paige picked up the cookie cutter, but she didn't cut into the dough. "Is saying 'it's not you but me' too cliché?"

That made him laugh. "It depends."

"On what?"

"Whether or not it's true."

"It is." She didn't hesitate to answer him. "If I was looking for casual fun, you'd be number one on my list."

His chest thrust out. Not what he wanted, but he'd take it. "Except you don't want that."

"I don't."

Wes forced himself not to flinch. He hated those two words.

"At the coffee shop, you mentioned not wanting to change your relationship status," she continued.

"I did, and I don't." Great, now he was saying it. "You, however, want what you told Santa. I mean, me."

She nodded, not an ounce of regret or remorse showing on her face.

Her certainty struck a chord inside him.

"I don't think I realized how much I wanted it until that day. I mean, I knew it in theory, but saying the words aloud to Santa like that..." A flush rose up her neck to her face. She blew out a breath. "I honestly never thought I'd be thirty-seven, single, and no date on the horizon."

He wanted to kiss away her frustration.

Don't even think about it, Lockhart.

"What did you think would happen?" he asked.

She half laughed. "That I'd get married after college. Then I was sure it would happen after med school. Then following my residency. Yet, here I am today, the same as I was each of those times. Still wanting something I can't have."

He understood how she felt. "There's nothing wrong with wanting to get married."

"No, but it's not something I can do on my own. Which is why I'm single. Finding someone who I'm compatible with, and falling in love is hard. I keep telling myself it'll happen, but not everyone is looking for forever."

"No, but you can't give up. Believing you'll find what you want is the first step," he encouraged, wanting to make her smile. "Staying focused is the second. But doing what's right for you is the most important. That's what you did with me last night, and it's how I've gotten through every challenge facing me."

"And made billions."

And got better with his healthcare team's help and a large amount of luck.

Wes nodded. "Keep at it until you get what you want."

She studied him like he was a lab specimen. All that was missing was a slide and a microscope. "You mean that."

It wasn't a question. "I do, even if it sucks for me."

She laughed. "Not for long. You'll be out having fun with your friends while I'm watching television or reading, trying to figure out a way to find a guy who wants the same things I do."

Wes knew she would succeed. "I would like to know one thing, but you don't have to answer if it's too personal."

"What is it?"

"You don't date casually, but how do you know if you want to have a relationship with someone if you don't go out with them?"

"So first off," she said playfully. "I've never gone on a first date and had the colors for the wedding picked out and our children named by the time we said goodnight."

"You wait until the second date?" he teased.

"The fourth or fifth," Paige joked. "I date the same as other people. Usually an initial meetup over coffee followed by a meal if we see each other again. But going out with someone not interested in having a relationship is a waste of time. That's what I mean about not dating casually."

"Makes sense." Knowing he fell into her waste-of-time category bristled.

"I wish I could meet someone, have everything click, and be in a committed relationship. That would be so much easier."

He thought about Adam, Kieran, Mason, and Blaise who'd married this year. All four had fallen hard and fast and couldn't be happier. "You need to fall in love at first sight."

She eyed him warily. "You believe that happens?"

"I've seen it with my friends."

Paige shrugged. "I'm not sure love at first sight exists. Other things could explain the immediate attraction."

"Wait a minute." Wes couldn't believe what she was saying. "You make wishes. You confide in Santa. Christmas magic is real for you. How can you not believe in love at first sight?"

"I don't know. Maybe I understand the chemical reactions in the brain that occur when two people are attracted to each other too well." Paige pressed the circle into the dough but left it there. Her face pinched. "Or maybe I've never met anyone who made me believe it could be true."

Her wistful tone gave him a glimpse of her vulnerability and her heart. Despite her words, she wanted to believe.

He forced himself to stay seated and not move closer to her. "Once you meet the right person, you'll know."

"Know what?" she asked.

When you know, you know.

Dash had said that. Maybe that was why things were working out so well between Wonderkid and Raina. "You are with the one you're meant to be with."

"I wish it worked that way. The truth is, I might be too jaded after trying dating apps and going on a few uncomfortable blind dates."

Wes's shoulders bunched. The image of her going out with total strangers set him on edge. What if the guy was dangerous? People joked about meeting axe murderers, but the news was full of scary stories.

"What happened?" he asked.

"I wouldn't know where to start." She sounded more amused than horrified. "Let's just say whenever we made it past the initial dates, my job somehow ended up getting in the way."

Paige deserved better. She needed someone who was supportive of the work she did. Not jealous of the time she spent helping her patients.

"You're smart and beautiful. Any man would be lucky to date you. Which tells me you haven't met the right guy yet."

"Thanks." She smiled softly. "Maybe I should forget what I've been doing and try something new."

"Like what?"

"Hire Hadley," Paige said matter of fact. "According to Raina, Hadley has an excellent success rate with her matchmaking service."

If anyone could help Paige, Hadley could. Wes's stomach churned. He sipped his coffee. That didn't help.

Wes didn't want to encourage her, but he had to say something. "They don't call Hadley the wife finder for nothing."

"Dash met Raina through Hadley."

"Yes."

"And you met someone, too."

Surprised, Wes lowered his mug. "Did Hadley tell you that?"

"Raina told me."

That was okay, then. Hadley promised to protect her clients' privacy, so he'd hoped she wasn't discussing him to Paige or anyone. "I only agreed to use Hadley's services out of my friendship with Blaise. I said I'd go out on one date, and I did. Nothing else happened."

Paige cut more biscuits. "Based on your experience, would you recommend Hadley?"

Wes's collar seemed to tighten. He swallowed. "Whether you want a wife or a husband, Hadley Lowell Mortenson is the best matchmaker in the business. She's expensive, but she's worth the investment if marriage to the love of your life is your end goal."

"Good to know."

"But Hadley's services can't be rushed."

"I'm not in a hurry." Paige placed the circles of dough on a second baking sheet. "I'm just exploring my options. To be honest, I can't see dating or having a relationship until the cancer center is underway."

That would be months from now. Relief surged through him. Not that he cared what she did. Okay, maybe a little. "You have time to figure things out."

She nodded. "I don't have years to wait, but birthrates have risen for mothers in their forties. So I'm not alone in waiting until I'm older. Though it is harder to get pregnant."

He assumed Paige knew that from her medical training, but maybe she'd been doing some research. He drank more.

"And if I don't find Mr. Right in the next year or two," she continued. "I can use a sperm donor."

Wes spewed a mouthful of coffee over the breakfast bar. He swiped his hand across his face. "Sorry."

She grabbed paper towels and cleaned up his mess. "Did I surprise you?"

More like shocked.

Until his diagnosis, Wes had thought little about being a dad, but his health care team, including Paige, had suggested he freeze his sperm before chemotherapy, so he had. Not that he planned to defrost those swimmers. "I wasn't expecting you to say that."

Her lips narrowed. "It's a valid backup plan if a woman wants children."

Which she did. Only Wes had thought kids were part of a bigger dream with a spouse, not something she'd pursue on her own. Having a baby wasn't like walking into an animal rescue and adopting a dog or cat.

He set his cup on the counter. "Yes…"

Her gaze pierced into him. "I hear a 'but' coming."

"But raising a child on your own is tough. Hadley's sister, Fallon, is divorced with two kids, and she's always exhausted."

She had moved her family to Portland from San Francisco with Hadley. All of them except Henry, who didn't work, offered Fallon a job. She chose the one with Dash's company. She was doing well there, but she also had Blaise and Hadley nearby to help as needed. Paige had mentioned her family was on the East Coast. Not exactly babysitting distance. But she seemed the type who could handle it better than most.

"Though if anyone could do it successfully, you could," he clarified.

"Thanks." Her gaze softened. "That's the nicest thing anyone has said to me."

"You've been hanging around the wrong people."

She laughed. "Maybe I have."

The timer buzzed. Paige put on an oven mitt and pulled out the biscuits. They were golden brown.

The fresh-baked aroma made his mouth water. "They look like Nora's."

Paige's face brightened. "I hope they taste as good as hers, too."

"I'll try one and let you know."

"Taking one for the team?" she asked.

"Always."

She placed a biscuit on a paper towel and set it in front of him. "It's hot."

"I'll be careful." Wes blew on the biscuit and then tore off a piece. He took a bite. Light, flaky, perfect. "Delicious."

Her smile widened. "Making them is easier than I thought it would be."

"Many things are." Wes ate more. "Trying something for the first time is the hardest part."

A thoughtful expression crossed Paige's face before she raised a brow. "Speaking from experience?"

He shifted on the barstool. "It's a piece of advice from Nora."

"A good one."

Wes nodded. Before being diagnosed, he never hesitated trying anything whether in business or his personal life. Now, a list of cons—all the things that could go wrong—crept up, which made him hesitate. Nora said he'd get over it. So did his therapist. But Wes wasn't as certain. He'd changed. Some differences made him better, but others, like this one, didn't.

"Do you follow it?" Paige's words held a challenge.

"Sometimes." That was as honest an answer as he could give. But it made him think. Nora had more common sense and street smarts than most people Wes knew. Maybe he should follow her advice.

Especially where Paige was concerned.

What was the worst thing that could happen?

An image of Annabelle flashed in his mind.

Nope. Not happening.

Wes blinked. Once, twice, until it disappeared.

Paige was different.

He enjoyed talking to her like this. They got along in a way he hadn't with another woman. Not since…he couldn't remember the last time.

All he needed to do was figure out what they could be to each other so he could see her again. Perhaps…friends?

He rolled the word over in his head.

Friends would be great.

Well, good.

Okay, better than nothing.

Yes, friends.

Wes only hoped Paige would be on board.

Guess he would find out.

Chapter Eleven

Coming home Sunday afternoon to an empty condo was surprisingly uncomfortable for Paige. Oh, she was happy to be back when she set her bag on the hardwood floor, hung her purse on the hook by the door, and removed her snow boots. But something felt…off.

Normally, she relished the silence following a busy day, but after the boisterous weekend in Hood Hamlet, especially the loud brunch that morning, the quiet irritated her more than it soothed.

Paige bypassed the kitchen and went into the living room, trying to understand. Everything was clean and in its place, other than the stack of boxes and bins of Christmas decorations and the stepladder she'd carried up from her storage closet. Even the philodendron was green and thriving. She touched the potting soil. Still damp.

"Hi, Phil," she said to the plant. The vibrant leaves brought a splash of life to the condo. "Miss me?"

That was when she realized what was wrong. She surveyed the living room from the comfy overstuffed couch to the full bookshelf. All the things she loved, but...

Paige missed having others around. No, it was more than that. She missed Wes.

Ridiculous.

Thinking about him—missing him—was not only silly but also stupid. Paige plopped on a chair. Logically, she knew that. Yet, she couldn't help herself.

This morning in the kitchen had been...perfect. She didn't even mind that he'd caught her singing badly. Though he'd been too much of a gentleman to say anything. Their conversation had flowed. No matter if the subject was difficult, talking to him was easy. Time flew. And...

Wes was mentioning something about the two of them when Nora interrupted him. He'd told Paige they would talk later, but that hadn't happened. Maybe he'd changed his mind about whatever he had to say or maybe it hadn't been that important.

A bummer because she liked Wes.

Really, really liked him.

As in, her crush was the biggest she'd ever had. Considering her infatuation with the Backstreet Boys when she was a teenager, that was saying something. If only…

Don't go there.

Crushing on him was one thing. But that needed to stop before she found herself with a painful case of unrequited love.

Wes didn't want a relationship. He'd said that multiple times. Not those exact words, but he left no doubt what he wanted and didn't want with a woman—with her.

Her brother, Ethan, had explained how men communicate. Literally, according to him. Allowing a revised fairy tale to form in her head, one where Wes changed how he felt about relationships, would be stupid.

Not. Meant. To. Be.

It was as simple as that. Disappointing, but neither of them was to blame.

"Still sucks because I've never gotten along with someone so well," she said to Phil. "Wes is also sweet and kind and hot. Okay, that's enough."

Because she knew herself.

Paige didn't think in terms of "oh, he'd be a good boyfriend." No, she jumped straight to "yes, he'd be a wonderful husband and father." No matter what she thought or felt about Wes Lockhart, she had to stop. Thirty-odd hours spent together—the longest she'd been with a person outside of school or work in years—didn't make them a couple or even friends. They'd made no plans to keep in touch when she left his lodge. Saying goodbye before she got in her car had been just that.

A farewell.

If he'd had something important to say earlier, he could have pulled her aside. Men like Wes and his friends didn't hesitate. They took action. That was how they'd made billions or married after only knowing a woman a few weeks.

She had no reason to be disappointed with how things turned out. Not with zero expectations going in. Discovering the quaint town of Hood Hamlet, seeing how Wes lived, and getting to know his friends who could help the cancer center would live in her memories long after this weekend.

Paige also couldn't forget how her toes curled the two times he'd kissed her. That didn't happen every day. Or ever, in her case. She should be grateful and was.

Now, it was time to put the weekend behind her. Real life was calling. Or would be once she recharged the battery. Paige removed her cell phone from her pocket and plugged it into the charger in the living room.

"The quiet will drive me crazy. We need noise."

Paige clicked the remote. A Christmas movie appeared on the television screen. Which reminded her of the biggest item left to do to prepare for the holidays.

"Now we can get this place looking like it's December instead of November or any other month of the year. I have a red bow to tie around your pot, Phil. No one gets forgotten during the holidays."

Her decorations had been sitting in the corner since Black Friday. She didn't want to wait another night.

"Decorating will be the perfect end to a wonderful weekend."

Only one thing would make tonight better…

Don't think about him.

Paige made herself a cup of peppermint hot chocolate before she carried a box to the couch. After unwrapping an ornament, she placed it on the coffee table. Each had a story, either the place where she'd purchased it or who had given it to her. She went through the first box and then the second while the movie played. This one, featuring a city girl doctor taking a position in a small-town hospital, was a favorite.

Her phone buzzed.

She glanced at the screen. Ethan had texted her. Given it was a Sunday, her brother must have a little free time. Maybe they could catch up. She had been too busy when he contacted her last.

Big Bro: *Are you watching Christmas Under Wraps?*

Paige: *Of course.*

Big Bro: *You enjoy imagining yourself as the doctor.*

Paige: *Well, yeah. Only I would have applied for more than one fellowship.*

Big Bro: *Maybe you should move to Garland, Alaska, fall in love with Santa's son, and get married.*

Paige: *I would except the place doesn't exist and neither does Santa, ergo there is no son for me to fall in love with and marry.*

Big Bro: *Wish you were coming home for Christmas. It isn't the same without you. Mom tries, but even when you were little you made the holidays come together for us.*

Paige: *Awww, thanks. I will be there next year. Promise!*

Big Bro: *Better idea. Move back to Vermont. The kids miss their favorite aunt.*

Paige: *I miss all of you.*

Paige's chest tightened. Her family didn't understand why she stayed in Portland. They kept asking her to move back, especially around holiday times. She wished they weren't on opposite coasts, but ever since coming west for her residency and fellowship, her life was here now. It wasn't as if she never saw them. She visited Vermont at least once a year. Sometimes twice.

She sipped her hot cocoa. No whipped cream, but the warm liquid went down smooth.

Her cell phone buzzed again.

Big Bro: *Where are you spending Christmas?*

Paige: *Not sure yet. I've had a few invites. Don't worry about me.*

Big Bro: *I always worry about you.*

Paige: *Says the man who tormented me when we were younger.*

Big Bro: *It was done with love.*

Paige: *Yeah, right. Just remember that when your kids go at each other. Karma, baby!*

Big Bro: *Mom and Dad already warned me.*

Paige: *I bet they did.*

Big Bro: *Seeing anyone?*

Paige: *Santa's son is handsome.*

Big Bro: *Someone not on your TV screen.*

Paige: *No. But I don't have time right now.*

Big Bro: *You have to make the time.*

Paige: *Maybe I would if I met someone who wants more than casual fun.*

Big Bro: *Do I need to fly out there and punch the loser for hurting you?*

Paige: *What do you mean?*

Big Bro: *Casual fun is not in your vocabulary. Assuming a guy said that to you.*

Paige: *Correct assumption.*

Big Bro: *If he said that, listen to him. There's no need to read between the lines. What he says is what he means.*

Paige: *You've mentioned that before.*

Big Bro: *It's true, so watch yourself. I don't want a jerk to hurt you.*

Paige: *I'm a grown woman.*
Big Bro: *You'll always be my little sis. Okay, kids are yelling. Using words they shouldn't.*
Paige: *Love you.*
Big Bro: *Love you, too. Talk soon.*

Paige plugged in her phone again and returned to the half-full box. In between sips of hot chocolate and watching the movie, she covered the coffee table with ornaments.

"Time for the tree." She rubbed her hands together.

Sitting on the floor, she removed the pieces from the box. The four-foot-tall artificial tree had lights attached to the branches, making the assembly easy-peasy. She put the tree in its spot, plugged in the light cord, and stepped away.

The white lights glowed. Pretty, but…

Paige rubbed her chin. Something wasn't right. She moved around the living room staring at the tree, trying to figure out what was bothering her.

The reason hit like a snowball to the head.

She'd had this tree for years, but today it seemed miniscule compared to Wes's and Henry's. The size had never bothered her before. She didn't know why it did now.

She didn't need a huge tree for herself. Someday, she would have the big, tall tree of her dreams—a live one that gave off a fresh pine scent, but the tree she had should work until then.

With the tree in place, Paige searched the coffee table for the pickle. The ornament was a family tradition, only she didn't hide it the way her parents did at their house. She attached the pickle to a branch before stepping back to admire the view.

Satisfaction washed over her. "Now it's ready for the other ornaments."

As she picked up a large silver bell—a gift from her niece—it jingled. Remembering kids at the hospital giving angels their wings, Paige shook it. The world needed more angels.

She hung the ornament on the tree.

The security buzzer rang.

Who would come to see her? She rarely got company. Someone must have hit the wrong unit number. That had happened before.

She pressed the intercom. "Hello?"

"It's Wes." He cleared his throat. "Can I come up?"

Wait. Wes was here? Her heart thudded.

"Paige?" he asked.

"I, uh, sure." She didn't know what else to say. "Two-oh-one."

Though if he'd called her unit, he knew that.

She pressed the button to unlock the main entrance. Questions threatened to overwhelm her.

Don't think. Smile.

A knock sounded.

She took two deep breaths before opening the door.

Wes had a smile on his face and her cape draped over his arm. "You forgot this in the guest bedroom."

Her stomach clenched. He wasn't here to see her but to return something she'd left. Paige shook off her disappointment.

"Thanks." Gripping the door handle like a lifeline, she pasted on a smile. "I haven't unpacked. I didn't realize I left it. I'm sorry you had to go to so much trouble."

She pressed her lips together to stop herself from rambling.

"No trouble. It's on my way home." He peered into her condo. "Nice place."

Where were her manners? Paige opened the door wider. "Would you like to come in?"

"Thanks." Wes walked inside and headed straight into the living room where he placed her cape over the back of a chair. "You're decorating."

"Hood Hamlet gave me a big dose of holiday cheer. I decided to stop procrastinating and get it done tonight."

Wes rubbed his neck. "I figured you were the type who put your tree up early."

"Usually, I do that." She remembered her schedule since Thanksgiving. "But I've been busy."

"Going away this weekend probably didn't help," he said with a hint of worry.

"No, but I enjoyed myself, and decorating won't take me more than a couple of hours."

He stared at the table covered with ornaments. "There's a way you could finish sooner."

"How so?"

"I can help you decorate."

A burst of excitement shot through her, but then she remembered what Ethan said. Wes, too. She shouldn't read anything into his wanting to help. "Aren't you tired since you didn't get much sleep last night?"

"I slept during the drive. Craig said I was out." Wes's eyes appeared brighter than they were earlier. "Must have been because I got a second wind."

She stretched her arm toward the ornaments. "Well, if you're offering…"

Mischief gleamed in his eyes. A corner of his mouth lifted in a lopsided grin. "I am."

She forced herself to breathe. "Okay, then. Grab an ornament from the table."

Wes removed his gloves and jacket. He wore the same sweater and jeans as he had on earlier, but she couldn't keep from sneaking a peek or two at how handsome he looked.

Oops. She probably shouldn't be doing that if she wanted to get over her crush.

He picked up a small teddy bear wearing a stethoscope. "Dr. Teddy?"

"Many of the ornaments were gifts. My best

friend gave the bear to me during my first year of med school."

Wes hung the hook on a branch. "Is she the one whose mom died?"

Nodding, Paige added a red ball monogrammed with a gold P to the tree. "We exchange more calls and texts than gifts these days, but no matter how much time has passed without talking, we pick up like we just spoke yesterday."

"She must be a special friend." He got another ornament.

Paige nodded. "You have an amazing group of friends yourself."

"I do." He held on to an angel. "I'm happy we've become friends."

"Is that what we are?" The question burst out before she could stop it.

He placed the angel front and center on the tree. "Given we want different things, being friends seems like the best option."

"Is there another?" she asked, half-serious.

He said nothing, but tilted his head, staring into the kitchen.

"I can hear your brain thinking from here," Paige joked, hoping to keep the mood light.

He laughed. "I can't think of one, but I had fun this weekend. I want to spend more time with you."

What he said shouldn't matter as much as it did, but she couldn't stop her smile from widening. "I'd like that, too."

He picked up a Santa. "Good."

Nodding, she wiggled her toes.

They continued putting the ornaments on the tree. The only noise came from the television. She didn't give the screen a second glance. The movie would be on some other time. Decorating the tree with Wes was real and happening now.

"I've only had real trees, but having the lights on the branches is a nice touch," he said.

She picked up a Santa ornament. "My family has real ones, but I decided to be practical. A pre-lit tree that doesn't drop needles makes life much easier, especially when Christmas is over. Besides, a fake tree is safer."

"Safer as in no fire?" he asked.

"Safer as in I kill plants."

"Let me just say, I'm glad I didn't know that when you were my doctor."

She laughed. "My grim reaper tendencies are limited to plant species, not humans."

"Well, that's a relief," he said playfully before pointing to the philodendron. "That, however, looks alive and healthy. Unless it's fake."

"Despite my efforts, Phil remains alive." As she stared at the plant, affection rushed through her. Any other person would feel pride except she had little to do with its survival. "A complete anomaly."

"Is that why you named the plant?"

She nodded. "The plant deserved a name after seeing all its succulent siblings be tossed into the garbage can."

His face scrunched in fake empathy. "Poor Phil."

"Poor me for unintentionally killing them."

"Traumatic." His voice was full of sarcasm.

"It was." Crossing her arms over her chest, she stared at Phil. "I thought they were cute."

"Cute things should live forever." Wes turned over the ornament in his hand to examine the back.

"I agree." Soon, only one thing remained on the table. "The angel goes on top."

He handed it to her. "I'll let you do the honor since it's your tree."

Paige placed the angel on top. Okay, the tree might be small, but it was pretty. "I love seeing the tree with all the decorations."

"What's next?" Wes asked.

"Decorations for the fireplace mantel and the lights that go around the two front windows."

"You do the fireplace. I'll do the lights."

She removed the picture frames and put a nativity set on one side of the mantel and a wooden family of snowmen on the other end. In the center, she placed red and white candles in glass cylinders and tucked fake pine boughs around them. Her stocking came next, hanging from a hook beneath the mantel.

Someday, Paige would have a real garland strung with lights, but this would do for now. She stood back and surveyed her work.

"Beautiful," Wes said.

"Thanks." She glanced his way. He'd finished one window, and he was working on the other. "Need a hand?"

"Could you hold the strand of lights?" He shook the dangling cord. "They kept getting in the way."

"No problem." Except the longer she stood there with him on a stepstool above her, bumping into her accidentally, the more of a problem it became.

Friends. Friends. Friends.

That became her new mantra.

"I've almost got it attached in the corner." As Wes reached up, he gave her a perfect view of his profile.

Her mouth went dry.

"Got it." He glanced down at her and smiled. "So what's next?"

Paige had no idea, but if he kept standing up there, she could put a Santa hat on his head, and he'd be a gorgeous addition to her holiday decorations.

Friends.

Paige blew out a breath. She had a feeling being friends with Wes would not be as easy as she thought.

Thank goodness she didn't have any mistletoe in one of her boxes or she would want to use it with her…friend.

Chapter Twelve

Sitting in the foundation's conference room on Wednesday, Wes ran over the latest report from Sadie, who sat across the table from him. The numbers blurred. He blinked and refocused.

His thoughts, however, kept wandering. The way they had since he woke up on Monday thinking about Paige. She was on his mind a lot.

The excitement of having a new friend.

That was all.

Speaking of which… Wes hadn't heard from her this morning. He glanced at the clock on the wall. Okay, it was only ten o'clock, but they'd been chatting and calling each other a few times a day. Paige usually sent a text by now. She must be busy. But he hoped she was as excited for tonight as he was. Wes had planned a special holiday surprise for her.

Sadie said something. Wes should pay better attention to what she was telling him.

Wait. He had been earlier. Maybe he'd missed a text or call notification while Sadie had been going over the report.

Wes flipped over his phone and saw many messages. As his pulse kicked up a notch, he unlocked the screen. Scrolling through the texts, he didn't see one from Paige. He slumped in his chair. All were from his chat group. That surprised him, given everyone was at work. Maybe hump day meant they were having slow mornings.

Dash: *New Year's Eve party at my place. 8:00 PM. RSVP to me or Iris.*

Mason: *Woo-hoo! Does this mean we'll be celebrating your engagement to Raina?*

Dash: *Seriously, dude. How does Rachael put up with you?*

Adam: *What do you need us to bring?*

Dash: *Nothing. Iris is taking care of everything.*

Adam: *Cambria and I need an Iris to run our household and cook for us.*

Dash: *Iris is awesome. I don't know what I'd do without her.*

Kieran: *You have the best housekeeper/chef, Dash. Selah and I want Iris.*

Blaise: *You'd better give her a big year-end bonus or one of us will steal her away from you.*

Dash: *I will, but she would never leave me.*

Henry: *Never say never, Wonderkid.*
Kieran: *Yeah, don't jinx yourself.*
Brett: *No, keep talking and jinx away, because Laurel and I want to hire Iris.*
Blaise: *First in line. Hadley loves Iris, too.*
Brett: *Get behind me and Laurel. Iris is a natural with kids.*
Adam: *I want in. Cambria and I love Iris's cooking.*
Kieran: *After me. Selah and I need Iris more than any of you.*
Mason: *Nope. End of the line. Rachael and I need help.*
Dash: *Dream all you want, but Iris is all mine.*
Blaise: *Hey, Wes is missing. Where is he?*
Mason: *Being examined by his sexy doctor.*
Dash: *Careful, dude, Wes is stronger than you.*
Henry: *Respect, Mason. Dr. Regis saved Wes's life.*
Adam: *They're just friends according to Cambria who spoke with Paige.*
Kieran: *Selah said the same thing to me.*
Mason: *Seriously? Just friends after the smoldering glances and hot kiss?*

Every family had that one kid who needed to keep his mouth shut. In their group, that was Mason. The guy had revolutionized the way people communicated digitally, but he could be annoying, saying whatever popped into his mind. Sometimes, that was a good thing.

Not today.

Wes hadn't planned on joining in the

conversation, but he had no choice unless he wanted the texts about him and Paige to continue. He didn't, so Wes typed a reply.

Wes: *JUST FRIENDS.*
Wes: *If I thought for a minute, I could lure Iris away from the Wonderkid, she'd be working for me already.*
Wes: *Dash - I'll be there on New Year's Eve. Thanks for the invite!*
Mason: *Will Paige be your plus-one again?*

Mason's question didn't deserve a response. Especially when Wes didn't know the answer.

Paige was on call over Christmas. He hadn't asked her about December thirty-first, but he wanted to ring in the New Year with her at his side. In his arms wouldn't be bad, either. With her lips against his.

His temperature shot up.

No big deal.

Kissing when the clock struck midnight was a time-honored tradition. That was all they'd be doing. Keeping a custom going. A kiss to usher in the new year was no different from a kiss under the mistletoe.

Maybe she would be up for one.

Did friends kiss that way?

He tried to remember Henry's New Year's Eve party last year. Iris had been there to help as she usually was when they had a group event. Wes didn't think Dash and Iris, who'd been best friends since they were kids, had kissed then or ever.

Dash had never implied anything like that ever happened with her. He was the least socially skilled among them, but he never held back. He considered Iris a friend only, and she didn't appear to have any issues with the women he'd dated over the years.

Wes had women friends. Sadie was an employee and a friend. His assistant, Eliza, too. But he'd never wanted to kiss them, or any other female friends.

Until Paige.

There had to be a reason.

And then he realized what it was.

They'd kissed twice, and the second time was better than the first. That explained why he wanted to kiss her again.

No big deal.

His phone buzzed, but he ignored it. Wes should focus on—

"So what did you think?" Sadie held her tablet.

He had no idea what she'd said. "Can you repeat that?"

Sadie's gaze narrowed. "I asked how the visit to the homeless shelter went yesterday."

"It was eye-opening, but I enjoyed helping." Since last week, he'd been going out with employees from the foundation when they visited organizations. The hands-on work made him feel good as if he was paying it forward in a meaningful way. He'd never realized how satisfying community service could be.

"I had no idea how much the shelter depends on volunteers. The place was overflowing with those wanting food and to get out of the cold, which got me thinking."

"Uh-oh. This sounds like it will be expensive," she joked.

"I can afford it." Increasing the amount he donated had been the plan for this Christmas, but he wanted that to continue throughout the year. "There must be a way to do more. A low-cost housing development, a jobs program, something to get people off the street so they can regroup and start fresh?"

Her gaze softened. "It's not a simple fix because of the mental health and addiction issues facing many homeless. There are programs out there—"

"Assign someone from your team to research them in the new year. Not you," he said pointedly. "You're supposed to be delegating these days."

"Will do." She typed on her tablet.

"I'd like to propose a community service initiative through all of WEL. Have the foundation find volunteer opportunities for employees. Strictly optional, but perhaps offer free food or a meal voucher for those who show up."

Sadie grinned. "You enjoy doing more than writing a check."

"I do." And he owed Henry for that. "Others will, too."

"I have the perfect person to head this up." Sadie placed her tablet on the table. "Are you going to tell me why you're so distracted today?"

"I just gave you two action items."

"Before that on your phone."

Busted. "I was answering a text."

She raised a brow. "From?"

"Dash."

"You get texts from him every day." Sadie leaned forward. Well, as much as her pregnant belly allowed her to. "What else is going on?"

A beat passed. And another. "Nothing."

Wes wasn't ready to discuss Paige. Not that there was anything to tell.

"It's not just today." Concern laced each of her words. "You haven't been this unfocused since you were sick."

"I'm healthy." He didn't want her concerned about him. That wasn't good for her or the baby. His former oncologist was having an effect on him, but not in the way Sadie meant. "There's no need for you to worry."

His phone buzzed.

Mason was no doubt being a smart aleck again. Unless Paige was between patients and had time to…

Wes glanced at the screen. It was her!

Paige: *Hope your day is going well.*
Paige: *Excited about tonight.*

She must have a full schedule today if it took her so long to text him, but hearing she was looking forward to his surprise tonight was worth the wait.

"Who is she?" Sadie asked, her voice full of curiosity.

Wes glanced up, disoriented. "What are you talking about?"

"Who sent you the text that made you go all heart eyes?"

Oops. He hadn't meant for that to happen. "A friend."

"Heart eyes." Sadie smirked. "Spill."

"It's nothing." No one would understand his friendship with Paige. He wasn't sure he did yet. His respect for her as his doctor had grown into something else, something special.

He enjoyed her company. Hearing her voice brightened his day. But it wasn't romantic as Sadie's tone implied.

A kiss on New Year's Eve was one thing, and even though he might be tempted, Wes couldn't cross the friendship line with Paige.

Yes, he was making amends for past wrongs and paying back the second chance he'd been given with his remission. But he was still capable of hurting others.

He would not hurt Paige.

And that would happen if he pushed things between them because he couldn't give her what she wanted—what she deserved.

But he would have fun spoiling his new friend.

Thinking about tonight, Wes smiled.

"Oh my goodness." Sadie's mouth dropped open. "You met someone. A woman."

He startled. He'd forgotten he wasn't alone. "Why do you think that?"

"The heart eyes were the first giveaway, but you have that dazed, slightly confused, totally infatuated expression that guys get when they're in love."

"We're not… I'm not…"

Sadie grinned smugly. "So there is someone."

"I…" Wes sighed. "Between you and Henry, I don't stand a chance."

"Henry is the master. I'm but an apprentice." Sadie's complexion glowed. "Who is she?"

"We're just friends."

Sadie wiggled her shoulders. "That's how it begins."

Wes leaned back in his chair, trying to be nonchalant. "There's nothing more going on."

"That's what they say, too."

He sighed. "I don't want to discuss this."

"Fine, but I'm here when you're ready." Sadie sounded almost giddy. "I'm happy for you. You're one of the best men I know. If anyone deserves to find a friend and love, it's you."

His heart sank because he knew better. He deserved nothing.

"Thanks." He croaked the word from his dry throat.

Sadie was one of the smartest people he knew, but she was wrong about him. Even if he wished she wasn't.

* * *

That evening, Paige sat in the back of Wes's SUV. Craig knew their destination, but she was clueless about "the surprise." She could tell they were heading east near the Columbia River. Wes had mentioned having dinner and said to dress warm, so she had.

Paige fought the urge to tap her feet to the Christmas music playing in the car. She forced herself not to ask any questions. Wes's pleased smile was enough to stop her from trying to spoil his surprise. Still, she was more excited than she should be for a meal out with a friend.

A friend.

She was trying to think of him as nothing more than her friend. Their daily texts and calls weren't out of the ordinary, but his occasionally starring in her dreams—romantic ones—was weird for a burgeoning friendship. Random thoughts of him popping into her mind didn't make much sense, either.

Leftovers from her crush?

Or maybe she was still crushing even though she tried hard to think about Wes as nothing more than a buddy or a pal.

Craig stopped at a well-known seafood restaurant. White lights hung around the roofline and doors. A life-size nutcracker sat out front.

Wes opened the back door. "We're having dinner here."

She'd had brunch there once. It was delicious food with a lovely view. "This is a wonderful surprise. Thank you."

He led her inside. The interior screamed Christmas with lights and decorations all over the place. They removed their hat, gloves, and coat before they started sweating.

"Lockhart, party of two," Wes said to the hostess.

A few minutes later, they sat at a table with a lovely view of the river and southwest Washington in the distance. The other tables were full. The din of conversation and laughter filled the air.

She studied the menu. "This is a seafood lover's dream."

"They have other items like steak or pasta."

"Seafood is fine." She set her menu on the table. "I know what I want."

"That was fast."

She shrugged. "A cup of clam chowder and the seafood cioppino sound good."

He lowered his menu. "I'm having a harvest salad and the grilled king salmon."

As if on cue, their server arrived with glasses of

water and took their orders.

"So how was your day?" Wes asked after the server left.

She sipped her water.

Protecting her patients' privacy limited what Paige could say. She wanted to tell him that Mr. Chaffey's nineteen-year-old grandson had been at her patient's appointment. She and Lydia had cheered after the two men left, but Wes didn't know the man or the backstory. Paige, however, was thrilled. A sprinkle of Christmas magic from Hood Hamlet must have made its way to Portland and the Chaffey family. She hoped this was only the beginning of the family getting closer.

There was something she could share. "I received a Christmas card from Dalton today. He was—"

"The little boy you colored with at Henry's party," Wes finished for her.

"You remembered." That surprised her given how busy he was running a company.

He nodded as if it were nothing, but it was, and her affection for him grew.

"How is he?" Wes asked.

"Dalton wrote he's feeling much better. He's also happy to be home with his family."

Wes leaned back in his chair. "Looks like he'll get his Christmas wish."

"Yes!" She lowered her voice. "His family has recovered, and he's so excited for the holidays. He said 'Santa is the man.'"

She agreed with the sentiment.

Wes's smile crinkled the corners of his eyes—the result had Paige taking another drink of water. "That's wonderful."

"It is." Thinking about the card surrounded her heart with warmth. "He sent me an ornament he made. It's hanging on my tree."

"Each one has a story."

"They do."

"I'd like to see your new ornament."

Her heart raced. "Anytime."

The server returned with their wine, soup, and salad. "Enjoy."

She scooped up a spoonful of chowder. "How was your day?"

"About the same as always only I had two meetings scheduled at the same time so that made things interesting." He half laughed. "Since I haven't found a way to clone myself so I can be in two places at once, I told Dash to work on that for me."

"Sounds like his kind of project."

Wes grinned. "He probably has a project like that going."

She laughed. "The chowder is tasty."

"So is the salad." He set his fork on the plate and sipped his wine. "I'm glad we could find time to get together tonight."

They'd both been busy yesterday and on Monday

night. "The holidays make schedules even crazier than usual."

"I have our company holiday party tomorrow."

"Will you be playing Santa there?"

"No, I gave the suit back to Henry, but I will announce the bonus for the year so I'm sure there will be some ho-ho-ho-ing." He raised his glass in a mock toast. "People should be pleased. At least I hope so."

"Rewarding employees must feel good. Giving money away how you choose. Bidding outrageous sums of money for a good cause. Making a donation that can change lives."

"It does." A thoughtful expression crossed his face, but the intensity in his eyes drew her in. "Unfortunately I didn't appreciate the ability to do that as much as I should have. I should have done more sooner."

"What changed?"

"Lymphoma." He wiped his mouth with a napkin. An odd mix of hope and fear gleamed in his eyes. "It was a big wake-up call to do better."

The emotion in his voice sounded sincere yet raw.

She covered his hand with hers. "You've done great things."

Lines creased his forehead. "And some not so good ones, too."

His regret tugged at her heart. She wanted to wipe away his sadness and put a smile on his face.

"No one is perfect. Everyone makes mistakes,

some larger ones than others, but all we can do is our best and be kind and caring and generous. You're all three, Wes Lockhart." She squeezed his hand, hoping to add her strength to his, because everyone needed a little extra sometimes. "Please don't think otherwise."

As an invisible cable seemed to connect them, the corners of his mouth lifted. "Thank you."

"You're welcome." Paige should stop touching him, but she had the feeling he needed the contact. So did she.

"Dinner is served," their waiter joked, but his appearance left Paige no choice but to raise her hand so her arm was out of the way. He set plates in front of them. "Enjoy."

The food was delicious. Conversation flowed as easily as the wine. Time seemed to fly, and the server was soon removing the dishes. He returned quickly with two peppermint hot chocolates in disposable cups. "It's almost time."

"Time?"

"Thanks," Wes said to the server before looking at Paige. "The Christmas Ships will be passing by. I ordered warm drinks. We can watch from inside or go outside."

An easy choice. "Let's go outside."

"The hot chocolate will keep us warm."

"You thought of everything." Paige smiled at him. "I thought dinner was the surprise. I had no idea there was more."

Wes winked. "There's always more. And it's usually the best part. Ready?"

Bundled up in their coats, hats, and gloves, they held on to their cups and stood on the deck. The temperature was cold enough their breath hung on the air, but Paige didn't mind. Even when a slight breeze off the water brought a chill, there was no place she'd rather be.

The fleet sailed by single file. Others around them oohed and aahed at the boats decorated with lights.

She sipped her hot cocoa. The liquid warmed her insides. "I love that they do this."

Lights outlined some boats. Others had a display or two. A few went all out with Santa and reindeer figurines.

She took another drink, relishing the heat sliding down her throat. "This is so fun. I would have never thought to come here."

"Cold?" he asked.

No doubt her cheeks were red. She sniffled. A runny nose was one of the hazards of being outside in wintertime. "I'll survive. Seeing the Christmas Ships is worth a shiver or two."

Wes stepped behind her and wrapped his arms around her. "How's this?"

"Nice." Paige didn't know if it was his body warmth or his being so close to her that warmed her up, but she wasn't as cold. She settled back against him.

"I agree." He tightened his hold on her.

She swallowed a sigh. It was all she could do not to lay her hands over his. Instead, she clutched her cup with one hand and tried not to touch him with the other. "I think I could get used to *more*."

His laughter rumbled against her ear. Her body was reacting oddly to him.

"Me, too," he said in a low voice.

Something brushed the top of her hat.

Not the wind. That almost felt like… Could it have been… Did Wes kiss her?

Paige didn't know the answer, nor was she going to ask the question, but this was her surprise so she would pretend he had.

And she was fine with him kissing her that way.

Maybe it was the cold or maybe it was Christmas magic, but a part of her hoped he would kiss her again.

With or without mistletoe.

And this time on the lips.

Chapter Thirteen

Watching the ships with Paige, Wes wished the holiday season could last forever. Her Christmas spirit overflowed and was contagious, but he didn't mind being exposed. Each of her gasps or sharp intakes of breath when a boat sailed past brought a smile. It also brought a dose of confusion.

Wanting to stand close to Paige—hold her—wasn't friend-like. Kissing the top of her head had been instinctual. She hadn't appeared to mind, so he wanted to do it again. That messed with his brain. Because if he were being honest, he wanted to kiss more than her knit cap.

After the last ship sailed by, they went back inside the restaurant with the crowd.

She yawned. "Excuse me."

"It's getting late." Wes hadn't noticed the circles under her eyes until now. He paid the check. "Let's get you home."

"Sorry. I was up earlier than usual, and it all just caught up with me."

"Don't apologize," he said. "Even doctors with superpowers and capes need sleep."

Paige laughed. "We do. Or at least, I do."

On the drive home, Christmas carols played, but Paige didn't sing along or mouth the words. When they reached the freeway on-ramp, she was asleep on his shoulder. Not that he minded being her pillow.

Her beanie had fallen halfway off. The scents of lavender and rosemary tickled his nose. The fragrance must be her shampoo. He sniffed. Yes, it was her hair, not her knit hat.

Her lips curved upward in a shy smile, suggesting she was having a pleasant dream. What about? Him?

Oops. That wasn't friend-like. Nothing tonight had been if he were being honest. The restaurant was perfect for dates. And that was what this had felt like—a date. A romantic one at that.

Maybe he needed to rethink what they should do next time they got together. There had to be friend activities out there. He thought for a moment.

Fishing.

Friends fished.

Only he hadn't been fishing in years. Not since a vacation to the South Pacific.

224

Board games.

Friends played games.

Only he hadn't done that recently. Not with the rash of weddings, though Dash kept talking about hosting a game night.

Movies.

Friends watched movies together.

Only he hadn't done that in a few weeks, maybe a couple months, but Paige loved Christmas movies.

That was it. He would invite her over to watch one. Netflix and…

Nope. They would watch as friends.

He was free on Saturday. Maybe she would be, too. They could do something before that.

Craig parked in front of Paige's condo building. "Do you want me to take her up?"

"I will." Wes hated waking Paige, but he gave her a nudge, anyway. "You're home."

She blinked open her eyes. Straightened. "I'm sorry I fell asleep."

"You needed it."

"I did." She stretched. "Thanks for the wonderful night."

"I'll walk you in."

He followed her into the building, up the stairs, and to her front door.

She unlocked it. "Do you want to see Dalton's ornament?"

Wes did, but he wanted to spend more time with

Paige. Awake or asleep didn't matter. He needed distance before he did something stupid like kiss her again. "I'll take a raincheck."

"It's late."

He nodded even if that wasn't the real reason. "Sweet dreams."

"You, too." She smiled at him.

His stomach did a somersault.

"I hope we can get together again."

"Me, too." He fought the urge to brush a stray hair off her face. One touch and he might need more. "I'm free this weekend."

Subtle, Lockhart.

Except did it matter if they were friends? This whole label thing confused him. Maybe they should just hang out together and not define what it was.

Her smile widened, but her eyelids were heavy. "On Saturday, I'll be finished at the hospital by eleven."

"We can discuss the details tomorrow." Wes touched her shoulder for a nanosecond before lowering his arm. "You need to sleep."

Nodding, Paige stared up expectantly as if she were waiting for him to kiss her.

Temptation flared. Heat flowed through his veins. He could think of ten different moves to make, but he didn't give in. "Goodnight."

Something flashed in her eyes, so brief he couldn't catch what it was.

She wet her lips. "Sweet dreams."

He hoped his dreams would be as sweet as her. "You, too."

Walking away shouldn't be as hard as it was. He didn't hear her door close, so he glanced over his shoulder. She stood in the doorway and waved.

Wes waved back before quickening his pace until he reached the SUV. He slid into the back seat that suddenly seemed ten times larger and lonelier without Paige next to him.

"Everything okay?" Craig looked in the rearview mirror.

"Yes." Wes's confusion had only gotten worse. Paige seemed to be throwing off mixed signals. Not that she was the only one. Maybe the adage about men and women not being able to be friends was true because he was having trouble thinking of her as only that.

The next day, Wes still couldn't figure out what he was feeling, but he wanted to see Paige. He also didn't want to wait until Saturday.

Wes: *Do you have plans tonight?*
Paige: *Yes, a staff party at the clinic.*
Wes: *Tomorrow?*
Paige: *I'll be free after seven.*
Wes: *Peacock Lane and dinner?*
Paige: *Sounds like a plan.*

On Friday night, Craig drove them along Peacock Lane, four-blocks of a residential street in southeast Portland decked out with Christmas lights and decorations, and then they grabbed a late dinner at an Italian restaurant. Once again, conversation flowed, no matter the subject. As they drove to her condo, Wes wished the night didn't have to be over.

"I'm stuffed from dinner." Paige rested her hand on the seat between them.

If Wes moved his hand three inches to the left, he could touch her. Ugh. He was getting borderline creepy. But he enjoyed being close to her, feeling her warmth and soft skin.

She leaned her head against the seat and touched her stomach. "Eating that slice of tiramisu was a mistake."

He laughed. "Tiramisu is never a mistake."

"I must have gained ten pounds."

Wes checked her out. He saw nothing different. "If you did, it looks good on you."

"When I can't zip my pants in the morning, I'll blame you."

"That's what leggings are for, according to Sadie, who runs the foundation."

Smiling, Paige nodded. "I have a few pairs of leggings. And they are great for those mornings I don't want to deal with a zipper."

Wes doubted that was often.

The image of her with a round belly like Sadie's

popped in his mind. Paige's face glowed. Something unfurled inside him.

Wait. What was he thinking?

Sweat beaded at the back of his neck. His muscles tightened into hard balls.

Wes shouldn't be imagining her pregnant. He shouldn't be thinking of her in that way at all.

Maybe he was getting sick. He ran his fingers over the lymph nodes on his neck. None felt swollen. But that fact didn't bring the usual relief. Not when the image of a pregnant Paige appealed so much.

She stared out the window. "After seeing Peacock Lane, I may have to add more lights to my condo."

"Nothing wrong with 'less is more' decorating."

She made a face. "But it's Christmas."

He thought about his house in Portland. "I have white lights along the roofline and a wreath on the front door. Maybe I should add one of those inflatable decorations like we saw tonight."

"If you do, the snow globe ones are nice."

"Not a character from a show or movie?"

"The snow globe ones remind me of a Christmas movie I saw."

She loved those movies, which reminded him. "Tomorrow after you're finished at the hospital, how does a tour of Pittock Mansion sound? Afterward, we can get take-out and watch a Christmas movie together."

Her lips formed a perfect o. "Yes, yes, yes."

Paige was adorable. "So that's a yes."

"Ha ha." She eyed him. "Did you think I'd say no?"

"No," he admitted. "But I would have sweetened the deal with peppermint hot chocolate."

"That is my beverage of choice when I watch holiday movies. What's yours?"

"I don't have one. I haven't seen that many."

She angled her shoulders toward him. "Which have you seen?"

He thought for a moment. "*Elf*, *Home Alone*, *A Christmas Story*, *Die Hard*, *Love Actually*, a few of the old classics."

"Any from Hallmark, Lifetime, Netflix, Disney Plus?"

He shook his head. "I never watched much TV until I got sick."

She rubbed her hands together. "You're in for a treat. Not everyone loves them the way I do. But we get along, so chances are you'll enjoy them, too."

They *did* get along. Wes couldn't remember getting along with anyone as well. It was as if they'd known each other for years. Okay, they had, but Paige being his doctor had been different than her being his friend.

Wes grimaced.

His head kept saying "just friends," but his heart disagreed. What had started as a whisper—*you need her in your life*—was growing louder—*you won't be whole without her.* But as soon as he was ready to follow his heart, his head screamed. "No, you *will* hurt her."

Did it have to be one or the other? He needed to figure that out.

Fifteen minutes later, he stood in front of Paige's Christmas tree. Funny, Wes smelled pine, but a fake tree wouldn't have a scent.

She pointed out a sparkly star. The ceramic ornament had been painted and decorated with glitter. "Isn't it sweet?"

Wes turned it over. On the back, he read the words written in black marker: *To Paige. I believe. From, Dalton.*

He didn't know what Dalton believed in—Santa or something else—but the big smile on Paige's face told Wes how much the ornament meant to her. That gave him an idea of what to get her for Christmas.

"Very special." Wes straightened the star. He noticed another silver star—the one from the dinner last week with her wish tucked in the back. Had she made a wish on Dalton's star, too? "You hung the ornament in the front where everyone can see it."

"Well, you and me." She stared at the tree. "I don't have many guests."

"I'm honored."

"We're friends."

Wes tried not to grimace. Being friends had been his idea and not his smartest, either. He was tired of what the word implied. And didn't. "We are."

But that was all they could be, right?

* * *

Paige finished rounds on Saturday morning. She stopped in the coffee shop to have a peppermint hot chocolate and a cranberry scone. That would tide her over until they ate after seeing the Pittock Mansion.

She sat at a small round table eating, drinking, and reading her email on her phone. She opened the personal ones from friends first. Some contained Christmas e-cards with letters telling her what was going on in their lives. Paige appreciated the updates. She'd never included a holiday letter in the card she sent the old-school way, using the U.S. Postal Service. Someday, when she had a family, she would write a letter. But who wanted to hear about her work and research?

A text notification beeped.

Big Bro: *Working or out having fun?*
Paige: *Just finished and about to have fun.*
Big Bro: *Doing what?*
Paige: *Touring a mansion decorated for Christmas with a friend.*

Except Wes felt like more than a friend. She'd caught him staring at her a few times. And for a moment on Wednesday, she thought he would kiss her. She didn't think she was blowing her crush out of proportion, but who knew?

Big Bro: *Is this friend male or female?*
Paige: *Male. His name is Wes.*
Big Bro: *When did you start dating?*
Paige: *We're just friends.*
Big Bro: *No guy looks at Christmas decorations with a friend. That's a date or you're his girlfriend or it's both?*
Paige: *Really?*
Big Bro: *Unless West Coast guys are different?*

Paige wiggled her toes. Maybe she hadn't been reading Wes wrong and there was hope for…more.

Paige: *I guess I'll find out.*
Big Bro: *Be careful.*
Paige: *Always.*
Big Bro: *Can you send Mom your recipe for spiced apple cider? Otherwise, she'll use the instant kind on Christmas.*
Paige: *Oh, no, she can't do that. I'll email it when I get home.*
Big Bro: *I hope things work out with you and Wes.*
Paige: *Thanks!*

She hoped so, too, because she enjoyed having Wes in her life. He was good for her and vice versa.

But one question kept her from getting too excited.

Had Wes really changed his mind about wanting a relationship?

* * *

This year's Pittock Mansion Christmas theme was the Wonderful World of Books. Eighteen rooms were decorated with an individual title in mind. The exhibit was popular, which meant Paige had little time to talk to Wes without others being around.

She didn't mind too much since she had wanted to see the decorations, but that left her no closer to figuring him out. Perhaps some covert studying of him might give her some answers. If not, at least she would enjoy the view.

"This is a lovely mansion." Poinsettias sat on the steps of the grand staircase. Fancy garlands hung on the banister. Beautiful, but… "It's hard to imagine a family lived here."

"Have you been to Henry's estate?" Wes asked.

She shook her head.

"It's not as old," he explained. "But his place has a similar feel. Laurel Matthews has been redecorating it room by room to make it more like Henry and less like his late parents."

That shouldn't surprise Paige, but sometimes she forgot his friends were billionaires.

The *Harry Potter* library captivated her. Little

touches from the series were everywhere.

"Look at the Hogwarts letters coming out of the fireplace." Wes typed on his cell phone. "Blaise will want to see this if he hasn't already. He's a huge *Harry Potter* fan. I'm sure Hadley's niece and nephew would love this, too."

Paige and Wes had read the books, so they took their time pointing out favorite items like the birthday cake made by Hagrid and the Marauder's map. They searched for as many "Easter eggs" as they could—as any true nerd would. Sharing the excitement with another fan made the experience so much better. The fact the person was Wes made her want to buy a lottery ticket tonight because luck was on her side.

They had more in common than she expected. She wanted to know everything about him.

Who was she kidding?

Paige wanted to date him.

She wished she was brave enough to ask him if he'd changed his mind about being just friends. The more time she spent with him, the more she fell for him. She couldn't stop herself.

But what if Wes said no to more? This was different than asking if he wanted a second dessert or another spin around the dance floor. Would he think she was pushing him? Would things change between them?

She didn't want that to happen, but she also couldn't stop thinking if they were this good as friends, they would be even better as a couple. That might be worth the risk.

Wes placed his hand at the small of her back. The gesture felt as natural as breathing to her. "Let's check out the music room."

Paige entered and found herself transported to another continent. "It's the *Madeline* room." A large Eiffel Tower lit up. She grinned. "Ooh-la-la."

"Paris is one of my favorite cities."

Of course he'd been there. Probably more than once. She forgot Wes could go wherever he wanted without a second thought. A nice perk to being a billionaire and healthy.

Once upon a time, when she was twenty-two and in college, Paige thought Paris would be a nice honeymoon spot. "I'd like to go there someday."

Wes glanced at her. "What's stopping you?"

"Time." She examined the table with place settings for each of the girls and dessert. "I spend my vacations with family."

And those were the vacations she actually took. The practice's office manager kept pushing Paige to take more time off. Maybe she should. Even if she went to Vermont again or just stayed home.

When they'd finished touring through the other rooms, Paige wanted to go through each again. She was certain she'd missed things. "Do you have a favorite?"

Wes shook his head. "I like them all. How about

you?"

"I can't pick only one." She ran through the various themes in her head. Cinderella, A Christmas Carol, The Secret Garden, Beauty and the Beast, The Joy of Cooking, and so many others. "They were all great."

She went with Wes to the SUV. Craig followed them.

"So dinner and a movie at my place?" Wes asked.

Excitement shot through her. She wanted to see his house. "Yes."

"What do you feel like? Thai, Chinese, pizza, hamburgers, Indian, sandwiches?"

All sounded good, but one stood out. "Hamburgers. I haven't had one in a while."

"Healthy eater?"

She shook her head. "The frozen ones don't taste the same as fresh."

He laughed. "I know just the place."

Thirty minutes later, they had picked up their food and arrived at his house. The neighborhood was one of the trendy addresses in Portland, full of high-priced Victorian and Craftsman-style mansions. His home, however, appeared to be brand new, with an urban feel. Lots of wood and glass, but minimalistic. Even the Christmas tree felt that way with white lights and a theme that matched the décor. The place wasn't warm and inviting like his lodge.

"Did Laurel Matthews decorate the place?" Paige

asked.

"No, I'm on her waitlist." He glanced around, not seeming impressed by what he saw. "I purchased the furniture with the place."

"Talk about move-in ready."

He nodded, motioning for her to take a seat on the couch. "It's not really my style, but I liked the location and floor plan."

She sat. "I love the openness and layout."

"That was a selling point, but making the space feel lived in has been an issue." He took the spot next to her and passed out their food. "I was so busy with work I didn't notice how sterile and cold the décor was until I got sick. Then, redecorating wasn't on my mind. Now…"

She picked up a french fry. "You're waiting for Laurel."

"Yes." He sipped his chocolate hazelnut milkshake.

"You have time."

He brightened. "Thanks to you."

"And many others on your healthcare team."

Wes studied her. "It's okay to take credit."

"I do, but I also don't mind sharing it."

As their gaze met, physical awareness buzzed through her. Her blood heated.

Paige raised her peppermint chocolate milkshake. The cold cup against her palm did little to cool her off. She sipped and then took a bite of her cheeseburger.

"I checked the schedule earlier. The movie starts in twenty minutes." He turned on the television, and the right channel came on. "I'll mute the sound for now."

She recognized the movie playing but concentrated on her food and Wes. "This tastes great. Just what I wanted."

He started to speak but stopped himself.

She noticed he had eaten little. "Is something wrong?"

"No, I just..." On the screen, a man cupped a woman's face before kissing her on the lips. Wes stared at Paige. "I had a great time today."

She smiled. "Me, too."

"And last night."

"Same."

"I said we should be friends, but we might want to rethink that." His words rushed out, one on top of the other.

Her heart beat triple time. "Rethink how?"

His forehead creased with what she took to be confusion. He could join the club.

"The line of friendship has blurred for me," he said.

Thank goodness he was braver than her. She forced herself to breathe. "I'm not sure where the line is myself."

He half laughed. "So that makes two of us."

Paige couldn't believe this was happening. Ethan was correct. Again. He would rub it in, but this time she wouldn't mind. "You said you didn't want to date."

"I did, and I'm not sure how I feel now. I know I want to keep seeing you." He picked up a french fry. "What if we don't label it for now?"

Wes hadn't said he changed his mind, but she would regret not taking this chance. "I'm fine not labeling it."

Not labeling us.

Wes had made one Christmas wish come true. Could he make that happen twice?

Chapter Fourteen

Wes's neck hurt. A weight pressed against him. His arm was numb. Even though he kept his eyes closed, he could tell he was sitting on the couch. The television must be on because someone was singing. Unless a choir of children was performing in his living room. He doubted Craig would go for that.

Wes blinked open his eyes.

On the screen, children wearing reindeer antlers performed on a stage. It was dark outside. He glanced at the clock on the wall—eleven. Still nighttime. They must have fallen asleep watching the second movie.

They.

That explained the weight and numbness.

To his right, Paige curled up against him, sound asleep as he must have been. Her hand, fingers splayed, rested over his heart.

Contentment spread through him. Even though she leaned against him, her head on his shoulder, there was a lightness in his chest.

This.

This is what has been missing.

Wes pulled her closer, but she didn't stir. He brushed his lips over her hair, something he'd been wanting to do for a week, inhaling the familiar scent of her shampoo.

He had money, power, and once again, his health. No matter how many times Wes told himself he was better off on his own, Paige had decimated those reasons with a smile.

He smoothed her hair with his hand. Silky soft.

More than friends.

Wes grinned, almost giddy. He had no idea what that meant, especially since they agreed not to label this—them. All he knew was that being with Paige felt right, more right than anything else ever had. And if he were truly honest with himself, he could sense Paige wanted to explore what they could become, too.

Did that scare him?

Yes!

His brain kept shouting all the reasons being more than friends was a bad idea. For well over two years, he'd listened to each and every one, especially after going into remission, but he couldn't with her.

He didn't want to, because being only Paige's

friend wasn't enough. He'd been kidding himself that was all they could be to each other. Whatever happened next, he promised two things:

1) To make the most of his time with Paige, enjoying her, spoiling her, helping her.

2) To not hurt her.

That should be easy enough, right?

She stirred, moving her hand and then her shoulders. Her eyes opened. As soon as her gaze met his, they widened. Her cheeks turned pink. "I fell asleep again."

"We both did."

"Your arm must be all pins and needles." Paige straightened. "That's better."

"No, it's not." He wouldn't let her go all doctor on him. He placed her on his lap. "This, however, is much better."

The pink on her face deepened, but she didn't disagree.

"So the movie." He smiled. "Do all feature a career woman from the big city who ends up in a small town for the holidays and falls in love with a nice guy who at first appears to be all wrong for her?"

"For a newbie, you catch on quick." She grinned. "There are a few variations to your formula, but they all end happily, too. That's the big selling point for me. I know exactly the payoff I'll get when I sit down to watch one and so do millions of others who enjoy them."

"What do you watch after the Christmas season ends?" he asked, curious to know everything about her.

"New Year's movies." A wistful expression formed on her face. "They are full of second chances like some Christmas ones, but wiping the slate clean and chasing your dreams in the new year are themes, too."

"I would like to do those things myself," he said without thinking.

"What's stopping you?" she asked, echoing his question to her about Paris.

Himself.

But he wasn't ready to say that aloud. Not even to Paige.

To do those things she'd mentioned, Wes would need to face his past and his demons. Something he'd never tried to do.

Could he do that?

He didn't know, but for Paige, maybe it would be worth a shot. Having a clean slate and perhaps a new label for their relationship come January first would start his new year off in a big way.

"I'll have to see what I can do," he said finally.

She beamed, appearing happy with his answer.

"Do the same movies continue all year long?" he asked.

"They have them for Valentine's Day, spring, wedding, summer, fall," she said. "But I don't watch many of those."

"You prefer the Christmas ones."

"I stop watching on January second."

Which meant she was a fan of the New Year's ones, too. Interesting. "Still, the networks must know their market well."

She nodded. "They have increased supply to meet the demand."

"Hearing you talk my language is a turn-on."

"I can think of a better way to do that."

Her flirtatious tone sent heat rushing through him. "How?"

Paige lowered her mouth to his and kissed him. She didn't hesitate or hold back. Her lips moved over his, telling him how she felt in ways she'd never voiced.

Wes was…

Home.

She was redefining what home meant to him, and he couldn't be happier about that.

He tightened his arms around Paige, pulling her closer. Her fingers ran through his hair. Forget the romantic kiss at the end of the movie they'd watched earlier. This kiss beat that one hands down.

Wes couldn't remember the last time he'd made out on the couch, but he wanted more. More kisses. More Paige.

Maybe he should add a second Christmas wish to his silver star—her.

He had no idea how long they sat there kissing. Time had all but stopped. But slowly the movement slowed, the pressure against his mouth changed, and then her lips were no longer against his.

Her breathing was unsteady. A hint of uncertainty gleamed in her eyes. After that perfect, rock-his-world kiss, the intelligent, capable, competent doctor was nervous.

Not for long.

Wes ran his finger along her jawline. "Things will work out just fine."

She nodded, but her concern remained.

He kissed her—hard and quick. "Trust me."

Her mouth curved upward. "I do."

Wes brushed his lips over hers once more. "Good. Because I have lots of plans for us."

Paige's blue eyes twinkled. "I like the sound of us."

"I like the sound of us much better than friends."

And he kissed her again.

* * *

Dreams do come true.

On Sunday, Paige woke up in her bedroom. She hadn't felt this rested in…forever. The sun shone through the edges of the blinds, which told her she'd slept in. That never happened, but she knew the reason.

Wes.

Thinking about him, her entire body smiled from the tips of her toes to her mouth. Her lips still tingled from Wes's kiss—the final one when he'd said goodnight at her condo's door. She would get another when they met for brunch in a little while.

Us.

She wiggled her toes. That was the best two-letter word in the English language. Second only to the best four-letter word…love. She sighed, thinking about what came next.

Merry Christmas, Paige.

This was the best Christmas ever.

Who cared if it was only the twenty-second of December? Santa had given her the perfect present—Wes. No wrapping paper, ribbon, or bow required.

Paige grabbed her cell phone off the nightstand to see if he'd texted her. He hadn't, but Ethan had.

Big Bro: *So…*

Shimmying her shoulders, she typed a reply. The wind must be blowing westward because Christmas magic was definitely in the air.

Paige: *You were right!*
Big Bro: *More than friends?*
Paige: *Yes! Squeal!*
Big Bro: *Happy for you, sis.*

Paige: *Thanks.*
Big Bro: *But be careful.*
Paige: *Always.*
Big Bro: *What are you getting him for Christmas?*
Paige: *Oh, I need to get him a gift?*
Big Bro: *Might be good to have on hand if he gets you something. Otherwise, awkward.*
Paige: *Will think of something. Thanks. Love you!*
Big Bro: *Love you, too.*

Paige crawled out of bed. Thank goodness for Ethan. It was weird she hadn't thought about buying Wes a gift, but then again, she didn't buy her friends gifts. And what could she give a man who could afford anything he wanted?

She tried to think of something but came up blank. This might take time. A good thing she had…

Three days to figure it out.

Okay, not that long, but they weren't spending Christmas together, so if she didn't see him before he left for Hood Hamlet on the twenty-fourth then she'd have extra time.

At eleven o'clock, she entered a café not too far from her condo. Wes sat at a table toward the back. He wore a forest green Henley and jeans. No man should look that handsome. Swallowing a sigh, she made her way to him.

He stood and greeted her with a kiss. "Good morning."

"Be careful," she teased. "I could get used to this."

"Having breakfast with me or a kiss?"

"Both," she admitted. "Though I'd take your kisses over food any day."

A grin lit up his face. "I'll have to see what I can do about that."

"Promises, promises." Paige sat. A menu was on the table in front of her, but she didn't pick it up.

"Know what you want?"

"Biscuits and gravy." Her stomach grumbled. "It's my favorite item on the menu."

"Then I'll have that, too."

A server filled their coffee cups and took their orders.

"I have a conference call at one."

"On a Sunday?"

He nodded. "But I want to see you later if you're free."

Her heart swelled. "Come over to my place when you're finished. I'll make dinner, and we can do something after that."

"A home-cooked meal will be a treat."

For her, too, since she didn't cook that often. Speaking of which… "If I burn dinner or it doesn't turn out right, we can order something."

"I have faith in you."

"I'll try not to disappoint."

He reached across the table and laced his fingers

with hers. "That's not going to happen. I…"

A startled expression settled on his face. Pressing his lips together, he drew back his arm, reached for his coffee, and sipped.

"What?"

"I'm glad you could meet me this morning." Wes's gaze dropped to the menu, and he stared at it as if he hadn't a clue what to order.

Except he'd told her he was getting the same thing as her.

Stop.

Paige needed to get out of her head and not analyze everything. She was here to enjoy his company. Nothing more. They were adults in their thirties. She was closer to forty. If something was wrong, he would tell her.

She raised her coffee cup. "So are you finished with your Christmas shopping?"

* * *

What was wrong with him?

After seeing Paige to her condo building, Wes slid into the back of the SUV. He had thirty minutes until the conference call, but that wasn't on his mind. No, something more serious was.

He had almost said "I love you" to Paige.

The realization stunned him, but he couldn't deny the truth. The words had been sitting at the tip of his tongue ready to cannonball out of his mouth.

Somehow, he'd stopped himself.

Thank goodness.

Once he said *them*, there were no take backs. He'd made that mistake with Annabelle, saying the words because he hadn't known how to reply when she said them to him. But love wasn't a *quid pro quo*.

Besides, this new thing between him and Paige was less than twenty-four hours old.

Wanting to say he loved her made zero sense.

He liked Paige. Liked her a lot. Liked her more than any woman he'd dated.

But love?

That was a far cry from just friends.

Non-label to love was a massive jump, too.

It was too soon. Way too soon.

When you know, you know.

But he wasn't Adam or Kieran or Mason or Blaise.

This thing with Paige had just happened. Wes wasn't looking for love. It was the last thing he wanted—deserved.

His hands sweated.

He removed his gloves and ran his palms over his jeans.

"Eliza texted me to remind you of the conference call," Craig said.

"Thanks." She had texted Wes, too. He had a feeling she'd also set an alarm on his phone somehow.

"We'll be home in time."

If they weren't, no one would start the call without him.

"Then you'll go back to Paige's," Craig said in a matter-of-fact tone.

As long as Wes could control himself and not think those three words again, he would go back.

Wait. Craig hadn't asked a question. "How did you know?"

The rearview mirror showed Craig's laughing eyes. "It's where I'd go if I were you."

A guess. Nothing more. Wes let out his breath. Chances were Paige hadn't known what he was about to say.

The garage door opened, and Craig pulled in. "Call me when you're ready to head out again."

Wes hurried inside to his office and sat at his desk. He'd have the call on his desktop and the info he needed on his laptop. Five minutes later, his executive staff was on the call with him.

"What's so important we have to talk today?" he asked.

Draper, a vice president, smiled smugly. "NanoNeu approved the buyout. The deal is a go."

The others cheered.

Wes understood their excitement. The technology would enable WEL to rise above its competitors. There was always a transition period, but the profits would be worth it. He spun a pen. "What about their employees?"

He'd never asked in the past. It had never crossed his mind. All he cared about were the potential profits and benefits to WEL. Anything else was…collateral damage.

"The technical team will remain in place. A few support staff." Draper might as well pick the canary feathers from his teeth given the way he gloated. "The rest are redundant staff."

Wes scratched his neck. "How many will be let go?"

Someone typed. Papers shuffled. Another person coughed.

He tapped his foot against the rug under his desk. Why was it taking so long? That number should be as important as any other in their data.

"Three hundred and eighteen," Draper announced.

Wes blew out a breath. "What kind of severance will they receive?"

Draper's forehead creased. "You've never cared—"

"I want to know," Wes interrupted.

"We'll get you those specific numbers on Monday." Kerri, another vice president, spoke up. "This isn't our first rodeo, as you know. WEL always provides a fair package."

Fair to those who would reap the rewards with bonuses, stock options, increased valuation, and happy investors. But was it fair to those who would no longer have a stable job and paycheck?

Wes scrubbed his face with his hand. "What's the timeframe for the deal?"

"First quarter twenty-twenty." Draper snickered. "We don't want anyone let go during the holidays, or Wes's reputation as a corporate marauder will be solidified."

People laughed.

"And this way they'll have a merry Christmas before they have to apply for unemployment," someone else added.

Wes clenched his jaw. His staff could see him so he schooled his features, but he dropped the pen before he snapped it in half.

"Not funny." He ground out the words. "Unless you want to see a severance package in your inbox, I'd learn to show a little more empathy and compassion for the people who will pay the price after their hard work made their company so successful."

Silence descended. The faces staring from his monitor paled. All muttered apologies.

"I want details of every package offered to NanoNeu employees on my desk Monday morning." His tone was harsh. He didn't care as he quit the call.

Acquisition talks had started before Wes went into remission. He'd barely been involved, but he hadn't stopped them. He'd encouraged the deal, not thinking of the repercussions—three hundred and eighteen employees.

Would buying NanoNeu help WEL?

Immensely.

That was all he should care about because he was helping his own employees with the deal, but he wasn't the same person he'd been.

Maybe Wes had gone soft. That was what his father would say. But what was wrong about caring?

Someone like Zeke, who needed medical coverage or another person, who lived paycheck to paycheck, might soon find themselves jobless. The stress of both situations was bad enough, then add in unemployment…

And there could be others like them.

Real people, who worked hard and struggled to make ends meet. Ones he'd met in waiting rooms or during chemo treatments or getting imaging. Ones not so different from him if his net worth disappeared. Ones who deserved recognition and rewards for their hard work.

For years, Wes had relished his cut-throat reputation, wearing it like a badge of honor. But now, he hated it. And when this buyout went through, even though WEL was buying NanoNeu not Wes himself, he would be the face behind the deal—the brilliant businessman people praised and the selfish billionaire they cursed.

No matter that he was only doing his job, maximizing profits for his company. Some wouldn't see it like that. And Wes didn't blame them one bit.

Because he wasn't doing more.

No matter how hard he wanted to change, to help others, to do better, he hadn't.

Not with work. Not with Annabelle. Not with…Paige.

They are full of second chances like some Christmas ones, but wiping the slate clean and chasing your dreams in the new year are themes, too.

He wanted to start anew in the new year with Paige, but he'd only been fooling himself.

His family had founded WEL. He'd grown up knowing running it was his legacy, and he'd thrived leading, expanding, and maximizing profits. This company was as much a part of him as his heart. He might not get the same satisfaction working as he once did, but he couldn't walk away. Wes had a responsibility to his family and his employees.

Not cancer. Not lo…

Wes shook his head.

Nothing would change.

Paige deserved someone worthy of her. Someone who could love her without freaking out just thinking the L-word. Someone better than him.

So how did he tell her?

Chapter Fifteen

Paige surveyed her kitchen. The scent from the cranberry pork tenderloin filled the air. The mashed potatoes and gravy were ready. The salad was in the refrigerator. Dessert was cooling on the rack.

Only one thing was missing—Wes.

The security buzzer went off.

Excitement shot through her. "Hey."

"It's me," Wes replied.

She hit the button to let him in and then hurried to get dinner on the table, nearly forgetting the rolls and butter. A Christmas-themed centerpiece and candles coordinated with her holly napkins and tablecloth.

A knock sounded.

Paige opened the door. "Hi."

She hugged him, but he didn't wrap his arms around her. Instead, he stood ram-rod stiff. "Wes?"

"We need to talk."

Uh-oh. That was ominous. "Dinner is ready."

"I… I can't stay."

"Oh." A weight pressed against her, making it difficult for her to breathe. "Is something wrong?"

He didn't answer, but walked into the living room. He glanced at the dining table for a nanosecond before staring at her tree. Usually, he took off his jacket. Not tonight.

Something was wrong. Paige tensed, her muscles tightening.

Don't borrow trouble. Her mom said that. Still, Paige chewed the inside of her cheek.

Wes handed her two envelopes, but he wouldn't look at her. "These are for you."

Confused, she stared at them. "It's not Christmas yet."

"They aren't gifts. I just…" His Adam's apple bobbed. "I want you to have them."

"Okay." But she felt anything but. As Paige opened the first one, her fingers trembled. Inside was a travel gift certificate. The number of zeroes made her do a double take. "Wes, I—"

"Go to Paris. Go to Vermont. Go wherever your heart desires." Wes spoke fast as if he might not get the words out. "It expires on December thirty-first of next year. I did that on purpose, so you won't put off your vacations until 'someday' arrives."

"I… Thank you?" Her voice sounded as shaky and uncertain as she felt. The amount would cover several trips for her and a travel companion, but Wes's tone suggested he wouldn't be going with her.

"Open the next one," he ordered with an edge to his voice.

The way he acted was so unlike him. Paige didn't understand, but she did as she was told. With unsteady hands, she raised the envelope flap and removed…papers. She unfolded them. The letterhead read "Matches by Lowell-Mortenson."

Wait. What is this?

The first two pages contained information about Hadley's matchmaking service. The next was a form. A questionnaire followed.

Paige lowered the papers. "I don't understand."

"You told Santa two Christmas wishes at the hospital."

"I did, but you made the most important one come true."

His gaze finally met hers. "I want you to have both."

Her heart leaped. If Wes wanted to take their relationship further that would be a dream come true but… She glanced at the papers. "What does Hadley have to do with making my wish come true?"

"She'll find you exactly what you want."

Paige was still missing something. "What I want?"

"A husband."

Her heart plopped to her feet.

"No one has the same success rate as Hadley. She's the best in the business."

Paige's shoulders sagged. Wes didn't want to be a part of her wish himself. He wanted her to date someone else. Marry someone else.

Her breath hitched. She clutched the papers. Tears stung her eyes. She blinked them away.

"I thought we…you and me…us…" Her voice cracked.

"There is no us." No emotion sounded in his voice or showed on his face. "It's not going to work out."

Maybe they hadn't put a label on what they were doing. And they had only been together a short time. But she hadn't mistaken the heat in his kiss. The desire in his eyes. The affection in his voice. "I don't understand."

His jaw jutted forward, hardening his expression. "I didn't mean to give you the wrong idea. Lead you on."

Lead you on.

The words reverberated through her and squeezed her heart like a vise. The pain, deep and unyielding. "You want me to hire Hadley—"

"I'm paying for it," Wes interrupted. "Fill out the paperwork and call her. You might be able to use the travel certificate for a honeymoon."

The words hit like a left jab. The air rushed from her lungs. Her heart shattered. But she had to say something, even if it hurt. "I wanted you to be my Christmas wish."

"I...can't." Something flared in his eyes. Regret, maybe? "You deserve better."

"You're one of the best men I know."

"I'm not. I've hurt people. I'm trying to do better, make amends, but it's not good enough. I don't want to hurt you."

Tears filled her eyes. "Too late. You're hurting me now."

He reached for her but then drew back his arm. "I'm sorry. I didn't want that to happen. Trust me, you're better off without me."

"How can I trust you now?" She blinked, trying to keep the tears at bay. "I don't know what happened today, but you're wrong. I've told you before, everyone makes mistakes. You. Me. No one is perfect. But that doesn't mean you have to rob yourself of happiness. Of...love. Please, Wes, let me help you."

"You're a great doctor, but you can't fix this."

Ouch. Paige winced. He didn't care about her the way she did about him, but her feelings hadn't turned off despite what he said. Whether or not he admitted it, Wes Lockhart was in pain.

"If you don't want my help, please reach out to your friends." She struggled to keep her voice steady. "You were given a gift—your life back when you went into remission. Not everyone gets that. Zeke didn't. You get the choice of what you want to do with that life. But making amends…"

She forced herself to breathe.

"You can give all you want, but if you're not giving for the right reasons, it won't make a difference. You'll be no better off."

A vein ticked at his jawline. "I'm giving for the right reasons. Paying it forward. Helping others. Giving second chances like the one I was given."

"You're not." Paige squared her shoulders. "Because what you're doing isn't about the recipient. The travel certificate, the matchmaking service… You're giving them to me so you feel better. Which is why that will never happen."

His nostrils flared. "You have no idea what you're talking about."

She couldn't stop now. "You need to forgive yourself for whatever you've done and move on. Otherwise, you'll spend your entire life trying to reach a destination that you can't find. It'll be a lonely journey, too. Because if you don't love yourself, how can anyone else love you? It may be a cliché, but it's true."

"You don't understand."

"I do, all too well," she admitted. "You have your health. More money than most people can imagine. And an incredible group of friends. Yet, you won't allow yourself to be happy. I hope someday you will.

Because you deserve happiness and love. So much love."

Wes started to speak but stopped himself. He turned and left her condo without saying a word.

The front door slammed.

"I love you." Her voice was raw. "Or I would have loved you if you let me. But sometimes love just isn't enough."

Paige wanted nothing more than to curl up into a ball and cry, but instead, she grabbed her cell phone. She pulled up her contacts and hit the first one that came up.

"Hey, Paige." The guy sounded like he was smiling. "What's up?"

"Hi, Dash," she said. "I'm sorry to bother you, but Cabot comes up before the others on my contact list first."

"You can call me anytime. Do you need money for the cancer center?"

"No, it's Wes." The tears she'd been holding back fell.

"Paige?"

"He doesn't want me to help him. He doesn't want me at all." She sniffled before pulling herself together. "He's not himself. He needs you guys, but I don't think he'll call."

"Where are you?" Concern filled Dash's voice.

"My condo. I'll be okay."

"I'm still rallying the troops," he said without

hesitation. "Someone will be at your place soon. I'm going to Wes's house."

"O-kay." Paige didn't know what else to say. "Please take care of Wes."

"I will. Promise." The clicking of a keyboard sounded in the background. "If you need anything before someone gets there, call me, okay?"

She nodded but then realized he couldn't see her. "Okay."

"Don't worry." Dash's voice soothed her. "This will all work out."

Paige didn't think it would. At least not for her and Wes. But she wanted him to be okay, whether that took a Christmas wish, Christmas magic, or a Christmas miracle. She prayed Wes got what he needed.

* * *

By the time Craig pulled into the driveway, Wes saw his seven friends standing at the front door. Anger flared. He slid from the car and strode straight to Dash. "I let you put your tracker prototype on my phone, but if you bugged—"

"Paige called." Concern filled Dash's gaze. "She's worried about you."

"Oh." That was the last thing Wes expected her to do. She should hate him, but then again, Paige wasn't like that. "Is she okay?"

"She's not." No judgment sounded in Dash's voice. "Hadley and Laurel are with her. The others are on their way."

Wes hadn't thought about Paige being alone when she was upset. More proof he wasn't good enough for her.

Dash tilted his head toward the door. "Let's go inside before we freeze to death out here."

"Please." Mason groaned. "It's cold. I need a strong drink to warm up."

They followed Wes into the house. Henry grabbed a bottle of whiskey and glasses from the bar. Adam pulled beers out of the refrigerator.

Dash removed a plate of snacks and a tray of Christmas cookies from a bag he had with him. "Iris put these together for you. They're all homemade, and she says you'll love them."

That was typical Iris. She could feed an army—well, the eight of them—with zero notice. "Tell her thanks."

Dash's mouth quirked. "You can tell her yourself."

Wes studied him. Maybe Raina was a good influence on him. "For someone we call Wonderkid, you're acting surprisingly like an adult."

"Sometimes I even surprise myself." Dash pointed to the couch. "Sit."

Wes did.

Within minutes, food and drinks were on the

coffee and end tables. His friends sat on the couch and chairs.

Dash lounged on the floor by the fireplace. "You broke up with Paige."

The great room went silent, but questions formed in Wes's friends' eyes. "She deserves a guy better than me. And before you come to my defense, it's not one thing but a combination."

All the men knew about his business reputation, which had kept growing more negative with each acquisition, but Wes took the time to do something he hadn't in the past. He explained to his friends how being thought of so negatively and leaving that legacy if he died had made him feel. And now that he was in remission, he had a second chance and wanted to change.

"I don't know if having cancer made me more touchy-feely or what," he admitted. "But it's not just acquisitions I feel differently about. Work just isn't the same for me. Which is strange, since that's been my life."

"It's because you're not the same, Wes. And that's okay," Blaise said. "Though I glimpsed the hard-nosed Wes in Las Vegas, so he's still inside you somewhere."

"What do you want to do?" Adam asked.

Kieran leaned forward. "Have you thought about resigning?"

"You have plenty of options," Brett added. "And

we can help you."

Wes knew that, but his friends were forgetting the most important thing. "WEL has been in my family for generations. I can't quit, but I don't know if I can keep working the way I have."

"Especially if it keeps you from dating the lovely doctor," Mason said.

Dash's face scrunched. "You called Paige sexy before."

"She's both," Mason explained.

"I can't believe I'm saying this, but let's leave Paige out of the equation for now," Henry said, his face tight. "I have a suggestion about your job, Wes."

Everyone, including Wes, stared at Henry with disbelief.

Henry rolled his eyes. "Okay, I haven't worked a day in my life, but I'm more than a social savvy billionaire with an impeccable fashion sense. I have a brain. You workaholics have surrounded me for years with your business talk and stuff rubs off."

"Let's hear what the trust fund baby has to say," Mason joked.

Brett shook his head. "Give Henry a chance."

"Thank you." Henry focused on Wes. "You've cut back at WEL already. Why not take it a step further? Make yourself chairman, hire a CEO and maybe an additional VP, and focus on your foundation. That's where you prefer spending your time these days. Work issues solved."

Wes's mouth gaped. So did everyone else's.

Henry smirked. "How did I do?"

Brett smiled proudly at his daughter's godfather. "That's a brilliant idea, Henry."

Everyone chimed in, talking over each other. Henry soaked up the attention and the praise.

He looked at Wes. "What do you think?"

"That I'll like my new title," Wes joked. "But seriously, thank you."

Adam passed Wes a beer. "Now, we need to figure out what you should do about Paige."

Remorse weighed Wes down. "It's too late."

"Never say never," Blaise said.

Wes stared at each of his friends. They'd supported him through his illness and were here with him now. Yet he'd kept something from them. Something big. He needed to tell them the truth.

Wes blew out a breath. "There's something I never told you."

"Dude, are your parents drug addicts, too?" Dash asked, wide-eyed.

"No." That would be easier if they had been. "This is about Annabelle."

Kieran's jaw tensed. "She's your past."

Nodding, Adam's face turned red. "Forget about the gold digger."

"I can't because…" Wes took a breath. "Everyone assumed Annabelle left me, so I let you all believe she was the one who broke up when it was me. I ended it. Broke her heart."

No one said a word.

Guess he should keep going. "After my diagnosis, Annabelle wanted to get married. All I could think was I had cancer. Why would she want me? I assumed she was trying to wedge herself into my life and take what she could, especially if I died. So I tried to make her prove herself because I just didn't believe she loved me. I broke up with her."

Kieran stared at the floor. "I got her fired."

Wes startled. "What?"

Kieran's complexion turned green. "I knew the owners of the boutique she managed. I told them what she did to you and got her fired. I figured that was the easiest way to get her out of Portland and away from you."

Wes stared dumbfounded. "I told you all to leave her alone."

"She hurt you," Kieran fired back. "Well, I thought she had."

"I had her evicted from her loft," Adam admitted. "I bought the building and forced her out."

Annabelle had loved living in that loft. Wes's insides twisted. He buried his face in his hands. "I thought she left Portland on her own."

"If it's any consolation, for once I listened and didn't seek revenge," Mason said.

"Me, either," Dash added.

"That makes three of us," Blaise said.

Wes shook his head. "This is all my fault. If I'd been honest from the beginning…"

"You had so much going on with cancer and WEL," Adam said. "I get it."

Kieran nodded. "I do, too. I wish you would have told us, but we made an assumption and you knew we would have been all over your case for breaking up with Annabelle."

Wes raised a brow. "Like you are now?"

Everyone laughed.

"I wasn't the only one keeping a secret," Blaise said.

"No, which is why I reacted badly when you told us yours," Wes admitted. "The guilt threatened to eat me alive."

Blaise hugged him. "No more secrets."

"No more," Wes agreed.

"You can't change the past no matter how much you want to," Blaise said. "But you can learn from it and move forward."

"I need to go to Seattle and apologize to Annabelle. Maybe then I can move forward."

"With Paige," Henry said a beat later.

"If she would give me another chance." But Wes doubted she would. Still, he needed to wipe the slate clean, literally. He glanced at the clock. "I'm going tonight."

"Two of us need to apologize, also," Kieran said.

Adam nodded. "I'm in."

"Except we have a problem." Wes sighed. "I

don't have Annabelle's address."

Dash tapped on his phone. Suddenly seven phones buzzed or dinged. "You have it now."

"Legally?" Wes asked.

Dash nodded, but the mischievous gleam in his eyes made Wes wonder.

"We'll need to take Henry's plane," Brett suggested. "Otherwise, all eight of us and those of you who travel with bodyguards won't fit."

"I contacted my flight crew." Henry spoke as if they were driving his car to the coast. "The plane will be ready to depart in an hour so let's get to the airport."

His friends went into action, cleaning up and putting away the food.

Wait a minute. Wes realized what Brett had said about why they were taking Henry's plane. "Everyone is going with me?"

Dash touched Wes's shoulder. "Like it or not, old man, but you're the big brother of this band of misfits. The glue that holds us together. Of course we're all going."

"If Wes is the glue," Adam said, his brows drawn together. "What am I?"

"Rubber cement," Henry answered.

Everyone laughed, including Adam.

Wes stared at each of his friends as they walked out of his house. "Thank you, guys. I don't know what I'd do without you."

Chapter Sixteen

Hadley, Laurel, Selah, Rachael, and Cambria spent Sunday evening with Paige, drinking hot cocoa, watching Hallmark movies, talking, hugging, and handing her tissues as needed. She needed many. Dash had told Raina to come to Paige's, too, but she had to pack so she stayed home.

Paige wasn't part of their group, but the women treated her like one of them. She appreciated their kindness and company. Nothing, however, stopped her heart from hurting.

How Wes acted upset her, but she worried about him, too. The others said to give him time, but Paige thought nothing would bring him back into her life. She only hoped his friends could help him—that he would let them help him.

Getting out of bed on Monday morning was tough. Her eyes burned. Her face was puffy. She thought about taking the day off, but the practice was short-staffed because of the holiday. All she had to do was be attentive to her patients and muddle through Christmas as best as she could. Not too much to ask.

She used makeup and eyedrops to hide the fact she'd been crying, trudged to work, and hoped the hours went by quickly.

Hadley, Laurel, Selah, Rachael, and Cambria each checked in with her, texting or leaving voice messages if Paige couldn't answer the phone. That helped her survive the day. Not an easy feat when she wanted to be in bed, but she did it.

For her patients' sake and for her own.

When she arrived at her building after work, Laurel and Noelle, wearing a pink snowsuit and strapped in a stroller, stood at the entrance.

"What are you doing here?" Paige asked.

"We brought you dinner." Laurel motioned to a large tote bag. "Shepherd's pie, a salad, and cookies."

Tears prickled. Saying thank you didn't seem like enough, but Paige said it anyway. "Thanks."

Laurel's eyes darkened. "I wish we could stay, but Henry needs me for something. Which, knowing him, could mean anything from putting away groceries to jetting across the country."

"Go have fun." With Henry involved, fun was a given. "I appreciate the dinner."

In the condo, Paige put the casserole dish and salad into the refrigerator. The cookies went on the counter.

Her appetite had been nonexistent, but she would get hungry, eventually.

This feeling wouldn't last forever. She would stop thinking about Wes. Time would heal her heart. The roller coaster of emotions would end someday.

Someday.

She bristled.

What had Wes said last night?

I did that on purpose, so you won't put off your vacations until 'someday' arrives.

His words swirled through her mind, sinking in deeper and deeper until…

Paige went into the living room and plopped on to the couch.

The more she thought about what he said, the more she realized Wes was one-hundred percent correct.

She put off things. Kept saying "someday" or "until then." Kept waiting until she had the perfect family of her dreams.

What if that family never materialized?

Family.

The word slammed into her like a runaway gurney. She said she wanted a family, but she already had one. Her parents, her brother, her sister-in-law, and their kids.

274

Paige had defined the mythical family of her dreams differently—a husband, a wife, and their kids—and centering her life around that definition.

That wasn't good.

Or right.

Especially when her family in Vermont hadn't been a priority since medical school.

Her shoulders sagged.

It was like a movie she'd watched where the heroine's life got off-track because she was focusing on a future that might not come true.

Paige loved her job. The cancer center was her passion, but she needed more than work. The weekend in Hood Hamlet had shown her that. Wes had, too. Now, her heart was onboard.

A feeling of lightness overtook her.

Forget making only one or two trips a year to Vermont. Paige would make the time, so she stopped missing out on holidays, activities, life with her family. She had a life to live—one beyond her patients and work. A life here, now, in the present.

Until Wes, she hadn't realized what she was doing.

Now that she did, she would take what he'd told her as a gift, the same as the travel voucher and paperwork from Hadley's matchmaking service, and make the most of it today and every day.

She stared at her Christmas tree.

Pretty.

For years, it had served her well.

Why did I need a larger tree when it's just me?

That was the line she'd told herself. Except it was wrong.

The fake tree was a symbol of her life, always waiting, putting off things until she had the life she imagined.

Stupid.

Nothing was guaranteed, especially the future. She knew that better than most. Yet she wasn't living in the present. She kept waiting, hoping, praying.

Stupid times two.

"I want a big tree." She moved the chair and end table, so the space in front of the window was clear. "It'll go right here. Well, once I get it."

Tonight.

She lived in Oregon, the land of Christmas tree farms and evergreen forests. Surely a tree lot in Portland had one left.

Two hours later, she loaded the seven-foot Douglas fir into the elevator with the help of a neighbor who took pity on her. Or maybe the guy was concerned for the tree. Either way, the tree ended up in her condo, filling the air with a sharp pine scent. No more fragrance sticks required. She placed the four-foot artificial tree on the other side of the fireplace and set up the tree stand. Twenty minutes later, she had it relatively straight.

"I think that's good enough, Phil." She studied

the tree from different angles. "Don't you?"

Paige put on the lights and beaded garland she'd purchased on the way to the tree lot. She had enough to get started and would add more decorations each year until she filled an entire tree.

Paige took off Dalton's star and the silver one from the dinner from her four-foot tree and hung them on the live one. She stepped back to get a better view.

Perfect.

For the first time in over twenty-four hours, a genuine smile spread across her face. Yes, things would get better.

* * *

On Christmas morning, Paige visited each patient in the cancer center. A few were alone, so she spent more time with them, but many were surrounded by family, which warmed her heart. She'd begged off dinner invitations from Blaise and Hadley, Brett and Laurel, and another doctor in the practice and his wife.

Paige wasn't in the mood to be social and jolly.

Her goal for the day?

To not drag others down because she was miserable.

To smile so nobody called her Scrooge.

To survive the holiday without bruising her

hurting heart more.

At lunchtime, she ate with others working today.

"Who is at home waiting for you?" a resident name Creighton asked.

Paige's smile faltered. She managed not to drop her fork. The temptation to say Phil was strong, but she thought better of it. The truth usually came out, and that would be awkward.

After her second round seeing patients, Paige went to the nurses' station where she worked on the orders for the patient in room 507. A chest infection had led to the woman being admitted. Yesterday, she'd showed signs of improvement, but today her condition had worsened. Paige updated the patient's treatment plan.

Shari, a long-time RN who kept the floor running smoothly, glanced up from her computer screen. "Dr. Barlow is looking for you. He's doing rounds and wants to speak with you."

Dr. Russ Barlow was a pediatric oncologist. "Patient consult?"

"He didn't say."

Nothing waited for Paige at the condo except for a few presents to open. The dinner she'd ordered from a grocery store wouldn't be the first Christmas meal she ate alone, but she hoped it would be her last. Next year, she would be in Vermont. No more putting off things for the future. She wanted to live in the present.

"I'll head over in a few minutes."

"I'll let him know." Shari returned to her charting.

Paige completed the patient notes and then logged off the system, so she could see what Russ wanted. She hoped nothing serious. December twenty-fifth should be a day for magic and miracles, not complications and problems. "Merry Christmas."

"Merry left the building three hours ago," Shari joked. "Enjoy what's left of your Christmas. We'll call if we need you."

"Do," Paige said sincerely. "I'm just down the street."

The sky darkened as she crossed the sky bridge. Snow fell, coming down faster than two hours earlier. All the Portlanders who'd dreamed of a white Christmas had gotten their wish.

So did you.

Yes, she had.

An imaginary band tightened around her chest. A reminder of what she'd gained and lost in two-and-a-half weeks. Such a short time that had felt much longer.

She'd received the official notification of Wes's donation to the cancer center yesterday. She was grateful, yet the timing hadn't been lost on her.

Christmas Eve.

Just like Santa Claus.

As she entered the children's hospital, she bypassed the elevator, taking the stairs instead. She couldn't shake the nervous energy bunching her muscles and jaw. Walking might help settle her.

Her footsteps echoed in the stairwell. When she arrived at her destination, the nurses' station was empty. Not surprising, but she didn't see Russ, either.

"Paige," a man called.

She turned toward the voice. Russ Barlow, a short man with a receding hairline, approached with quick steps. "Merry Christmas."

"Merry Christmas to you," she said. "You wanted to see me?"

A sheepish expression crossed his face, deepening the lines around his mouth. "Sort of."

"It's a yes or no question."

Russ rubbed his hands together. "Follow me."

She did, but... "Are you okay?"

He nodded, looking stressed, and led her to the entrance to where Henry's Christmas party had been held. "He made me an offer I couldn't refuse. I hope you understand."

"Understand what?" The room was dark. "He who?"

"Please go in there. That's all I ask." Russ hurried away, his shoulders hunched.

Paige had no idea what was going on, but she stepped inside.

It was empty from what she could see.

A Christmas tree lit up. The white lights glowed, showing her she wasn't alone. Sitting in a large chair was Santa Claus. Not any fill-in Kris Kringle.

Wes.

Paige's heart slammed against her rib cage. She sucked in a breath.

He made me an offer I couldn't refuse.

Russ's words now made sense. Paige crossed her arms over her chest as if that could protect her from… She had no idea what, but she needed to do something. "What are you doing here?"

"Wishing you a Merry Christmas. I also want to say I'm sorry," he said. "Hurting you was the last thing I wanted to do, but I did it anyway because I'm an idiot."

"You had your reasons."

"I did, and I mean it, which is the other reason I'm here."

"Shouldn't you be at your parents' house?"

"Yes, but there is somewhere else I need to be. Some place more important."

"Where?"

"With you." His gaze pleaded with hers. "I want to spend Christmas with you."

"Wes, I…" She inhaled deeply. "I've been worried about you. If this is your way of saying you're okay, great, but you hurt me."

"Paige, I—"

"Let me finish."

He nodded.

She took another breath. "Yesterday, I realized

you were correct. I haven't been living fully in the present. I've been putting things off, waiting for some imagined future when my dreams have come true. I keep saying 'until then' or 'someday' instead of going after what I want. No more. I won't wait any longer."

"Good, because that's why I'm here." He stood. "To go after what I want, but…"

Paige didn't want to ask, but she couldn't stop herself. "What?"

"I've been afraid." His voice was full of regret. "That's kept me from living in the present, too."

"What are you afraid of?"

His Adam's apple bobbed. "I worry the cancer will come back."

That was a real fear to patients and their families. "We spoke about this at your last appointment."

A guilty expression crossed his face. "I might have told you I was handling it better than I was."

Concern ratcheted. "Are you still seeing the therapist?"

He nodded. "The appointments are helping, but if I get tired or I catch a cold and a lymph node swells or a hundred other little things, I think it's back. I'm not sure if I'm making up or exaggerating symptoms or if something is real. It's…"

"Exhausting?"

"And paralyzing."

She wanted to soothe his fears. "You can't help how you feel. The fear of a recurrence is real. I wish it wasn't. Could the cancer return? Yes. Will it? I hope not because no one wants to go through that again. But you are healthy now. Try to focus on that instead."

"I've been trying." His gaze clouded. "But I don't want to be a burden if I get sick again."

Her heart hurt for him. "You have never been a burden, Wes. Taking care of someone is a way to show love and compassion and kindness. Your friends stepped up because they love you. That much is clear from the time I spent with them. You are all a family. And you're the big brother, the patriarch. They look up to you."

"I don't know why. I've torn companies apart without a second thought for their employees. I made decisions that affected thousands of lives without considering the consequences."

"That's why you're so hard on yourself?"

He nodded.

"You may have been that guy once, a man who only cared about the bottom line, but you're not him now. He never would have donated twenty-five million to the cancer center. He wouldn't have gone to a toy store to pick out gifts for a benefit dinner and grabbed three extra requests from the giving tree. He wouldn't have gone out with his foundation or done so many other things big and small."

Wes stared at her with an unreadable expression in his eyes.

"You can't change the past," she continued. "But you're not doing what you did anymore."

"I'm not. I resigned as CEO. I'm now the chairman."

She had no idea what the different roles meant, but… "You sound happy about the change."

"I am. It was Henry's idea." Wes smiled. "I've been trying to be a better man, but once you came into my life, I wanted—want—to be someone you respect."

"You already are, Wes."

"There's something else." He cut the distance between them with purposeful steps. "I lied about Annabelle. She didn't break up with me. I broke up with her. I didn't believe she loved me even though she wanted to get married. I thought she was only after my money. That she could never love me with the cancer. But worse, I let everyone think she broke up with me. I had the perfect chance to apologize when we were in Hood Hamlet, but I couldn't do it."

His anguish clawed at Paige's heart. "It's never too late to say you're sorry."

"I told the guys. And then we flew to Seattle on Sunday night," he admitted. "I finally apologized to Annabelle."

"How did she take it?"

"Better than I thought she would." His expression softened. "Annabelle is married and pregnant with their first child—a boy. She was as shocked to see me in Hood Hamlet as I was to see her, so she wasn't sure what to say. Her long parka hid her stomach, and she was wearing gloves so I didn't see her wedding ring. She forgave me and said what happened turned out for the best. She's madly in love and happily married. Her future son now has an educational trust that three of us will fund."

"Telling your friends and seeing her must have been hard to do."

"I should have never gotten myself in the situation, but a lesson learned." He scratched under his fake beard. "I'm learning lots of those."

"It's called life."

"Paige."

"Wes," she said at the same time.

They laughed.

"You go first," he urged.

"No, you."

"Okay." He sounded slightly winded. "Neither of us has been living in the present. You've focused too much on the future. I've been stuck in the past. You want to change, and so do I. Let's work on it together."

Her heart roared in her ears. "As friends or…?"

"You are my friend, but you're so much more than that. When all this started, I wanted to make your wishes come true, but you did that for me. Wishes I was too afraid to admit to until I met you."

Joy overflowed from her heart.

"You made me reassess everything," he continued. "I have work to do, but I'll do whatever it takes to be a man you can love."

Her pulse skittered. "You already are."

His face lit up. "Really?"

She nodded.

"I want you in my life. Today, tomorrow, forever." He reached into his pocket and pulled out a blue box tied with a white ribbon. "This is for you."

"I didn't get you a gift."

His tender gaze felt like a caress. "Yes, you did."

Her insides trembled. So did her hands, but she opened the lid. Inside was a crystal heart ornament. "It's beautiful."

"My heart belongs to you, but I thought you could hang this on your tree."

Each one has a story.

So did this ornament. Christmas magic? Yes, she believed.

"Thank you." She held the box to her heart. "I'll treasure it always."

"There's one more thing I want to give you." Wes reached into his pocket again, removed another blue box, and kneeled in front of her.

She gasped and covered her mouth with her hands.

"I love you, Dr. Paige Regis. You are an amazing

woman who saved my life when I was sick and saved my heart when I was well. We haven't been together long, but a good friend told me when you know, you know. I know you are the one for me."

He opened the box and showed her what was inside. A big—the largest she'd ever seen—diamond sparkled.

She lowered her hands, still trembling, from her face.

Wes gazed into her eyes. "Will you do me the honor of being my wife?"

"I love you." Her heart beat fast. She tried to slow her rapid breathing. But she had a feeling it would take a while. But she didn't want to leave him hanging. "Yes! Yes, I'll marry you."

He slid the ring onto her finger. A perfect fit.

Wes stood, pulled the fake beard below his chin, and kissed her.

"I've never kissed Santa before," she teased.

"There's always a first time." He kissed her again. "And a last one. Unless the Santa is me."

Contentment flowed through her, settling around her heart like a well-needed hug. "Thanks for making my Christmas wishes come true."

He caressed her face. "Thanks for making wishes so they could come true."

She pressed her lips against his, a kiss full of her love and respect for the man she would marry. "Now what?"

"If you don't have other plans tonight, I want to introduce my fiancée to my family." Wes hugged her. "How does that sound?"

"Like a wonderful way to spend our first Christmas together."

"It will be." Wes brushed his lips across the top of her head. "But just wait until next year."

Epilogue

New Year's Eve

The party was in full swing by the time Dash arrived home—three hours late because of a delayed flight from Boston. He should have spent Christmas at home, but Raina had wanted him to meet her family. Nice folks, but now he was unfashionably late to his own New Year's Eve celebration.

Ignoring the music, conversations, and laughter drifting upstairs, Dash showered in record-fast time to wash away the travel grime and dressed in the jeans and shirt Iris had laid out for him. He didn't know if Raina had arrived yet, but she would find him. She was like ferrous metal to his magnet.

Downstairs, Dash searched for who he wanted to see most. Well, two people.

Making his way through the crowd, he greeted his friends. A DJ played tunes. People danced. Despite his late arrival, everyone appeared to be enjoying themselves, because Iris had everything under control, as usual. Dash didn't know what he would do without her.

In front of the living room's twenty-foot-tall Noble fir Christmas tree, he found who he was looking for. Wes stood with a silly smile on his face, making heart eyes at his fiancée. The weight he'd been carrying around on his shoulders was gone. He appeared ten years younger.

Maybe laughter wasn't the best medicine—love was. It appeared to have worked miracles with Wes.

His friend falling in love thrilled Dash. He nudged Wes's arm. "I hear congratulations are in order."

"Thanks." Wes hugged him. "Paige saying yes was the perfect Christmas gift."

Dash raised a brow. "How long did you date?"

"If you count the night we reconnected at Henry's Christmas party at the children's hospital, two-and-a-half weeks," Paige answered.

"Adam and Cambria have you beat. He proposed a week after meeting her. And they married two weeks after that."

Wes nodded. "I thought Adam was crazy, but when you know…"

"You know," Dash finished for him.

Wes laughed, wrapping his arm around Paige. "You really do know."

"Great." Except what did a person know exactly?

Dash enjoyed being with Raina, more than he had with any other woman he'd dated. They were a good match, sharing similar hobbies, interests, and values. She was everything Dash never thought he would find, but thanks to Hadley Lowell Mortenson, aka The Wife Finder, he was now Raina's boyfriend. At least that was what she'd called him in front of her family.

Dash wasn't at the heart eyes stage. Being apart from Raina for days didn't bother him. Even though marriage came up at her parents' house, wedded bliss wasn't on his radar.

Not everyone was like Adam, Kieran, Mason, Blaise, and Wes. Love could take time to develop. That happened with Brett and Laurel Matthews. Maybe that explained why Dash didn't know if Raina was the "one" for him yet.

The cork popping from a bottle of champagne interrupted Dash's thoughts. He smiled at Paige. "Let's see the ring."

The lovely doctor's face glowed. She raised her left hand.

Dash whistled. "That's a humongous diamond."

"Wes picked it out." Paige leaned into her fiancé. "But it's too much."

Wes kissed the top of her head. "You deserve only the best."

Her cheeks reddened.

"The two of you look great together." Dash would have made a toast in their honor except he hadn't been to the bar yet. "Have you set a wedding date?"

Paige stared at Wes with such affection Dash felt like a third wheel. "We're in no rush to say 'I do.'"

"I'm not like the others," Wes said. "We want to have a long engagement. Paige needs to focus on the cancer center, and I need to work on myself a bit."

The others had married within weeks of proposing, but Wes had never followed the crowd.

"How long will you wait?" Dash asked.

"No idea," Wes admitted. "I proposed because I wanted her to know I was in this for the long haul. For forever."

Dash envied his friend's certainty. He felt that way about work but never another person, including Raina. Then again, he wasn't good at socializing or dating, but she didn't seem to mind when he was too busy and forgot to text or call.

Paige wrapped her arms around Wes. "You made your intention clear, my love."

Add one more friend to the crazy-in-love column. At least Dash could count on Henry Davenport to be eternally single. The guy dated so many women, he didn't know the meaning of commitment or, if he did, he avoided it.

"I'm happy for you guys." Their engagement thrilled Dash. Wes was the backbone of the group. If anyone deserved to fall in love and live happily ever after, he did. "But it looks like I'll win the bet now."

"You don't win until I say the words 'I do,'" Wes reminded him. "Who knows? You might beat me to the altar."

A shiver ran along Dash's spine. "Not going to happen."

"You caught the garter at Blaise and Hadley's wedding. That means you should be next if the tradition holds."

Dash shook his head adamantly. "Still not happening."

"We'll see." Wes smirked.

"What's that supposed to mean?" Dash asked.

"You spent Christmas with Raina's family in Boston. That's taking the relationship to another level."

Dash flinched. "It is?"

"Yes," Paige and Wes said in unison.

Dash scratched his chin. He'd said yes to the trip because Raina asked. His mom and dad were both going out of town for Christmas, so there was no reason for Dash to be in Portland. But he hoped he hadn't given Raina the wrong idea that he would be the next one to propose.

"The gears are cranking in Dash's brain," Wes

explained to Paige. "The lines on his forehead are a dead giveaway along with the way his mouth twists."

Blaise clapped his hand on Dash's back. "Nice of you to show up at your own party. We heard your flight was delayed."

Dash nodded. "I told Raina we should have left yesterday, but she wanted to spend more time with her family."

"Did you propose on Christmas like Wes did?" Blaise asked.

Say what? The thought hadn't crossed Dash's mind. "Nope. And marriage isn't on my five-year plan."

"Then make sure you don't give Raina the wrong idea," Blaise said.

Wes laughed. "Marry a matchmaker and now you know everything about relationships."

"Marriage teaches you a lot." Beaming, Blaise glanced across the room to his wife. "About your partner and family."

"How was your first Christmas with Hadley?" Paige asked.

"Amazing. Fallon, Audra, and Ryder were there. Lex, Rizzo, and Iris, too."

Wait. What? Hearing Blaise's bodyguards had been included in the celebration didn't surprise Dash, but he hadn't expected Iris to be there. "Did you hire her to cook Christmas dinner?"

A weird expression formed on Blaise's face. "Of

course not. She helped Hadley and Fallon with the food, but she was there as a guest."

"A guest?"

Blaise nodded. "We didn't want her all alone in this big house on Christmas."

All alone.

As the words reverberated through Dash, his stomach dropped to his feet.

"You forgot Iris has no family," Blaise said matter-of-factly with no judgment in his voice.

No one but Dash. He struggled to breathe. He was the worst friend ever. She always spent Christmas with him. On the twenty-fourth, they ate dinner with his dad. On Christmas morning, they went to his mom's house. In the evening, they exchanged gifts before eating while watching a movie. That had been their tradition for years.

Until Raina.

Dash swallowed around the snowball-sized lump lodged in his throat. "I forgot."

"That happens when you fall in love," Paige said.

Love? Was that the reason? Dash had no idea. He'd bought Raina and her family gifts. Well, Iris had purchased, wrapped, and shipped them.

His heartbeat roared in his ears. Dash hadn't bought Iris a present. No doubt there would be one underneath the tree for him from her. Had he even given her a bonus like he usually did? He didn't think so.

"Don't worry about it." Wes smiled at him. "Iris understands."

Dash nodded because Iris always understood. Since they met when they were thirteen, she'd forgiven him for doing stupid stuff, but that didn't make him feel any better.

"Did she have a good Christmas with you guys?" he asked.

"Iris did," Blaise said without missing a beat. "She spent Christmas Eve at our house so she could be there when Audra and Ryder woke up. Christmas is more fun with kids around."

"Thanks for taking care of her." Especially when that was Dash's job. He wanted to smack himself.

"Anytime, though Henry was the one who looked after her the most while you were away," Blaise said.

"He's claimed Iris's kiss at midnight," Paige added.

"Henry?" Dash stared at his friends. "As in our Henry? Henry Davenport?"

"The one and the only." Wes laughed.

Iris was an adult capable of making her own decisions. She could kiss whoever she wanted when the clock struck midnight. Those kisses meant nothing.

Except Henry was a player. The guy could break her heart before January second arrived. Dash didn't want that to happen.

"I'm going to grab food," he said, knowing Iris

would be in the kitchen. "I'll talk to you later."

He didn't wait for a reply.

At the entrance to the kitchen, Dash stopped.

Not only was Henry in there with Iris, but the guy also had his arms around her. Henry acknowledged Dash with a brief nod and a devilish grin before kissing Iris.

Not a peck or a brush of his lips.

A full-on kiss.

Make that kisses.

A knot formed in Dash's stomach.

What was going on?

It wasn't midnight, but Iris didn't appear to mind being kissed.

"Hey." Raina sidled up to Dash. "I've been looking for you."

Dash forced his gaze off Iris and Henry. "I didn't know if you were here yet."

"I hurried over." Raina touched his face. "What's wrong?"

"Nothing." The word shot out hard and fast. Dash couldn't keep from glancing into the kitchen.

Henry was still kissing Iris.

Dash's blood ran cold. Iris being kissed shouldn't matter.

It didn't matter.

"You sure?" Raina asked.

Not trusting his voice, Dash nodded, but he wasn't sure about anything at the moment.

The new year was supposed to be his best ever with a thriving company, friends who were happy and in love, a bet that was his to win, and a perfect girlfriend.

He stared at Iris and Henry still kissing.

So why did everything suddenly feel...off? Wrong?

And what was Dash going to do about it?

The Deal Breaker

The Billionaires of Silicon Forest, Book Three

There are some lines friends should never cross…right?

Status quo might as well be Dashiell Cabot's middle name. He has a job he loves, a billion dollars in the bank, and a best friend named Iris who keeps his personal life running smoothly. Why would he ever want to change any of that? But when Iris Jacobs tells him she's quitting and returning to culinary school, Dash's beloved status quo is thrown into chaos. Even worse? The thought of her departure is forcing him to realize his feelings for her might extend beyond the friend zone.

Iris wants more out of life than taking care of Dash. She always has. And even though she could never repay him for everything he's done for her, she can no longer afford to protect his precious status quo at the expense of her own dreams. She has no choice but to leave…unless he can give her a compelling—and possibly romantic—reason to stay.

They've always been just friends. That was their deal. But when all is said and done, something will be broken—either their deal…or their hearts.

About The Author

USA Today bestselling author Melissa McClone has written over forty-five sweet contemporary romance novels. She lives in the Pacific Northwest with her husband, three children, two spoiled Norwegian Elkhounds, and cats who think they rule the house. They do!

If you'd like to find Melissa online:
www.melissamcclone.com
www.facebook.com/melissamcclonebooks
www.facebook.com/groups/McCloneTroopers
twitter.com/melissamcclone
www.instagram.com/melmcclone

Other Books
By Melissa Mcclone

STANDALONE

A matchmaking aunt wants her nephew to
find love under the mistletoe...
The Christmas Window

SERIES
All series stories are standalone,
but past characters may reappear.

The Billionaires of Silicon Forest
The Wife Finder
The Wish Maker
The Deal Breaker

Quinn Valley Ranch
Relatives in a large family find love in Quinn Valley, Idaho...
Carter's Cowgirl
Summer Serenade

Beach Brides and Indigo Bay Sweet Romance Series
A mini-series within two multi-author series...
Jenny
Sweet Holiday Wishes
Sweet Beginnings

Her Royal Duty
Royal romances with charming princes and dreamy castles...
The Reluctant Princess
The Not-So-Perfect Princess
The Proper Princess

Printed in Great Britain
by Amazon